MW01230934

Enjoy

The Secret *of the* Old Red Bridge

by Cora A. Seaman

Cora A. Seaman

2/10

Disclaimer:
This story is purely a work of fiction. Any reference to names and people, whether living or dead, is coincidental. The 'Old Red Bridge' actually sits in an area near the Indiana line. I chose it as a backdrop for the story from my very fertile imagination.

Cover design by David Branstetter
Layout by Aztec Printing, Inc.

Editing by Don A. Seaman

Cordon Publications

731 C. Erie Ave.
Evansville, Indiana 47715
www.cordonpublications.com
Cora@cordonpublications.com
(812) 303-9070

First printing: October 2009.
Printed in the United States of America
ISBN 978-0-9822083-6-6

Acknowledgements:

This book is dedicated to my good friend, Lois Rini, who searched and found the bridge that had been a part of her memory from her early years of living in Posey County. Her inspiration and encouragement have been quite instrumental in the setting of this story.

Dedication

I owe my corrected grammar and sentence structure to my husband, Don, who spends hours poring over my manuscripts to prevent me from being an embarrassment to my early schooling in a one-room schoolhouse. I am eternally grateful for his willing spirit and spiritual guidance.

THE SECRETS OF THE OLD RED BRIDGE

Chapter one

Hannah knew that her sons had helped her survive when there was no one else to assist her in plowing the fields, harvesting the crops, and tending the animals. She also considered them her partners in keeping the farm producing since these chores were so important to their survival. In addition to her sons, Taylor had been a tremendous help to them when times were hard. Lydia, though just a child, was like a mother hen protecting her flock, was the helpmate inside the home, and all of them managed to survive without an adult male present in the home. Bartell had not been around for several years. The War had taken him away from them in 1861. Hannah had watched as he walked away from them. He had ridden off on their only horse when a squad of soldiers from the Indiana 154th Regiment of the Union Army rode up to small cabin. He had told her goodbye and that he would return soon. He left her in charge of their meager little farm in Griffin, her children, two cows, chickens and a pair of mules, to survive against all odds until he returned.

Anytime that she drove the wagon across the old covered bridge, glancing between the slats on the side into the swirling water below, she paused for only a moment as she considered the events of the past. Then she drove the team of mules on toward town.

Back on the farm, Luke was busy working in the barn trying to repair the harnesses and getting ready to plow the same plot of ground that he had already been working since he had been tall enough to guide the plow and mules. He was the 'true' farmer of the family, and he had learned all the ways to create enough food on the farm to support his family. Someday he would look for a wife, but not today!

John had always been the studious one in the family. He was usually found in the hayloft reading a book, a habit that nearly drove his mother crazy. He performed his chores only when she demanded. Otherwise, he read anything that he could find in their tiny little community to read. When he accompanied his mother into town for supplies, he always wanted to know where he could find another book or newspaper to read. She usually had to browbeat him into helping her get the supplies in the wagon before he went exploring for additional reading materials.

Mark was nowhere to be found on this sunny day. He was the hunter in the family. He had managed to learn the skill of hunting shortly after his father left for the War. He was only 8 years old when Bartell left, but he was big enough to shoot a gun. He practiced in the woods behind the house until he became a 'crack' shot at shooting something for supper. In the winter when the vegetable supply for their dinner table would be nearly gone, Mark would bring home a wild turkey or a rabbit for the family to enjoy without the benefit of potatoes or turnips. His fishing prowess nearly compared to his hunting skills, and he often caught fish from the creek that ran under the old covered bridge near their home.

Lydia was the lone female in the family besides Hannah, her mother. She was a beautiful but fragile child. She did not have the stamina to fend off the cold weather needed to work in the barns or hunt with her brother Mark. However, she was very good at baking biscuits or making bread for their evening meals. In addition, she was becoming quite an accomplished seamstress. She was the youngest of the family, having been born after her father had left for the war.

This was a blessing in disguise. A family secret had been kept from her most of her life. Because she was the only girl in the family, her brothers tended to her every need and most of her requests. In addition, the boys wanted to protect her from every suitor that attempted to make friends with such a lovely lady. The family lived together in a rather crude cabin nestled in the far corners of their farm in rural Posey County near a town called Griffin.

JOHANNA
Or Hannah as she was called.

Chapter two

Hannah Alstadt had been born in 1834 to parents who had lived in the same community for generations. They were poor but proud, God-fearing people who eked out a living from a meager piece of bottom land near the creek bed. She had had several siblings, but only one other child survived through those early years. Hannah was the only girl survivor and her mother never understood why she did not get another boy who could help on the farm. Hannah's mother was convinced that she would be able to handle the household chores, but more men were needed to tend the farm. It did not seem to matter how hard Hannah tried, she could never please her mother. She would hibernate in the barn where her father and brother were working hoping to learn what they were doing and become needed as an additional helper on the farm. However, her father always said she should be in the house doing "women's" work. In her heart, Hannah did not feel needed anywhere.

Hannah's mother and father were an ill matched pair. From how Hannah saw them, they seemed to be at odds all the time. Her father never seemed to be pleased with anything her mother did. In addition, her mother constantly nagged him about his 'filthy' habit of chewing tobacco. Somehow, Hannah did not seem to think that it was a sin to chew tobacco. She sympathized with her father's point of view that her mother did not seem to do things to suit anyone except herself. Hannah regularly watched, as the arguments seem to escalate every evening around bedtime. The wrangling would continue into the times that they were in bed together.

Hannah and her brother, Sewell, had slept on a cot in the kitchen. Nevertheless, the arguing could easily be heard all over their tiny little cabin.

Chapter three

As time went on, Hannah grew into a beautiful young woman. Her hair was a light auburn that turned golden in the summer sunlight. Her finely chiseled features gave her the aura of a china doll. Her slender frame would have been more beautifully draped if she had been dressed in a finer wardrobe. However, the family had little money for frivolous things, so Hannah wore the clothes that were left from her mother's wardrobe. She lacked the feminine skills that most girls her age were taught at home. Her mother did not teach her how to sew or embroider. Her mother was convinced that those skills were only for the aristocracy. Hannah had no idea as to who that might be, but she longed to know how to make herself a new dress rather than be forced to wear the ones handed down to her. Most of the clothes that she inherited were nearly threadbare. They fit her slender body with a gunnysack look. Hannah knew that, if she had a chance, she could learn many things that a woman should know, but there was no one to teach her.

Sewell was a hard worker. He worked beside

his father on their farm. The work was demanding and the crops were slim, but the family seemed to be able to survive on what they could raise on their little plot of ground. Sewell often thought that it might be best that the other children had not survived. How would they ever have had enough to feed three more children?

Hannah grew into a lovely girl without much help from her mother. She never knew why she could not please her mother, but she realized that no one else seemed to please her either. It became quite obvious to Hannah that her mother might have loved them, but did not like anyone including herself. However, Hannah did not understand what the root of her mother's unhappiness might be.

As the family continued to survive and times became a little better in the community, some social activities became evident. On Saturday night, a group of people would gather in the town square and have a party. It did not take much to instigate a party, but some of the men had fiddles, which they gladly tuned and played for the crowd. The women would wear their finer dresses, which usually meant a clean one rather than a dress with any finery on it. The event became a weekly get-together for all the community.

The Alstadt family always tried to make it to the town's party. Hannah especially loved the parties. They gave her an opportunity to meet other young people and to get to know something about other families in the surrounding farms.

Sewell loved the opportunity to mix with the other young men who were eagerly watching the young girls. Sewell knew that he wanted to find a wife and marry soon. He aspired to having his own family and getting away from the constant wrangling that was going on at his home. He vowed that he would never cause his wife the troubles that his father caused his mother. At the same time, he was sure that any wife that he chose would not nag him, as his mother did to his father. Surely, his married life would be more peaceful and pleasant than what he saw his parent experiencing at home.

Hannah surveyed all the other young women at the Saturday night parties and saw that some of them had learned how to wear their hair in curls rather than in braids as her mother insisted that she must wear. Some had fancy combs in their hair. Some wore nice bonnets with ribbons on them. Some had high button shoes. Hannah had none of these accoutrements. She only had braids, felt hats left from the men, and work shoes. She wondered how and where she might get these other fineries.

Hannah gathered with the other young women and listened to them talk about the young men. She heard them discuss the socials that were often held at the church. She knew that if she went to the church with them, she might also learn how to get all the finer things that she wanted in life. Maybe she would even find a husband there and get away from the drudgery that she was enduring at home.

When she returned home that night, she inquired of her mother if she could attend the church services the next day. Strangely enough, her mother did not object to her attending church if she promised to get her chores all done before leaving, and if she would take her brother Sewell with her for protection. Instantly, Hannah sensed that the problem in getting Sewell to accompany her might be an obstacle. She hurried to the barn and presented her case to him, explaining that there probably would be women there for him to meet. After a bit of cajoling and promising him future favors of extra pie or biscuits, Sewell agreed to take her to church the following Sunday.

Chapter four

Hannah arose very early in preparation for her visit to church. She prepared the breakfast for the family and cleaned the dishes in record time. Instantly, her mother insisted that she prepare their noon meal before she could leave. Hannah hurried to the cellar and picked a large piece of cured meat that she could put on the stove with potatoes in it to cook while she was gone to church. She left the bread dough to rise, knowing that the dough would become ready to knead while she was gone. She quietly 'hoped' her mother would do that for her. She swept the kitchen and the porch, hung up the dishtowels on the line, and believed that she had fulfilled all the requests that her mother had made on her before she went to church. As she and Sewell crossed the old bridge on their way to church, she looked down into the water. The water looked cold and impersonal. It was running fast on down stream to some place unknown to Hannah. She wondered where it ended. Did the water go on forever? If she dropped her hat in the water, would it disappear forever? She wondered.

Chapter five

The worship service at the church was a new experience for Sewell and Hannah. There were several people in attendance. The preacher spoke of a story from the Bible. It fascinated Hannah. She did not know much about the Bible. Her father read the Bible at home, but never out-loud, so she had no knowledge of what it said. He prayed a blessing at mealtime, but it was always the same, and Hannah assumed that all families said the same prayer at mealtime. To Hannah, this was a ritual and it did not mean much.

As she and Sewell rode home, she began to ask him questions about the service. What had Sewell learned, she wanted to know. He only replied that Hannah was right. There were several young ladies in attendance, and he could probably have his pick.

"Did you like the preacher's story?" she asked.

"What story," Sewell replied.

"Didn't you hear what the preacher was saying about Jonah and the great whale?"

"I never believe that stuff; it's just a story."

12

Hannah sat back on the wagon seat and thought about all the things that she had heard. She listened to them singing songs that she had never heard before, and she listened as the preacher read from the Bible. She wondered if her father would let her read his Bible. Then she realized that she could not read.

So many things to learn! How to read! How to get finer clothes? Could she ever learn good manners?

The road home seemed too short for her to comprehend all the things she wanted to understand before she reached the 'pit of anger' again.

Chapter six

When Hannah and Sewell returned home from church, their lunch was nearly ready to be put on the table. Hannah's mother had finished kneading the bread and had baked it in the oven for their noon meal. However, her mother was very angry that it had taken so long for them to get home. When Hannah tried to tell her about all the exciting things that the preacher had talked about, her mother refused to listen to what she was saying. Hannah really wanted to talk about the church service. Hannah's mother wanted to talk about what she had left undone during the morning. Hannah looked to her father for some support, but he just sat silently. She asked Sewell if he would explain what the preacher had been talking about during the service, but he only smiled and continued to eat his potatoes.

Hannah cleaned the kitchen after their noon meal was finished, and made the necessary preparations for their evening dinner. She filled the oil lamps and trimmed the wicks so that there would be better light in the evening. The air was still a little cool so she brought in three logs for the fireplace and laid a fire, but left it unlit, knowing that her father would light the fire if he felt that it was needed. She also brought in wood for the morning fire to fix the family's breakfast. As soon as she felt that she had her chores completed to the satisfaction of her mother, she asked her father for the family Bible so that she could try to learn to read it. He refused her request saying that it was too hard for her and that she should remain in the kitchen with her mother.

Hannah was disappointed that she could not get her father to allow her to read his Bible. She was so enthralled with the happenings of the morning and her experience at the church service that she was determined not to be discouraged. She vowed to herself that she would learn to read somehow and then she would be able to read the Bible as well as any other books she could find. In addition, she made a promise to herself that she would return to the church as often as she could. She was soon going to be turning 14 years old and she wanted to be treated as a grown-up. She did not want to be treated like a child any longer. Even though her mother insisted that she do the hard work in the house, and her father refused to grant her the privilege of learning to read, she knew that she would soon be able to make decisions for herself.

Hannah hurried to the barn to find Sewell. She wanted to talk to him about the girls that he had met at the church. She found him in a stall milking one of the cows. She began to ask him questions about one of the girls that she had seen him talking with, before they had left to come home.

Sewell was not very talkative about what he had experienced at church. He was afraid that his father would not approve of his meeting girls. Sewell had heard his mother and father discussing the fact that their two children would need to stay at home with them to help tend the farm. If they thought that Hannah or Sewell were meeting other people, they might not allow them to participate in any of the activities at the church or even in town.

Sewell loved going into town for supplies so that he could meet and talk with other people in the area, but his father would forbid it if he thought that Sewell was fraternizing with other men or women. The Alstadt parents were terrified that their two children would somehow find a way to leave them and all the farm work would fall on them to do alone. It frightened both of them to think that they might end their lives alone.

Hannah continued to ask Sewell more questions about the young girl that he was talking to at the church. As he continued to milk the cow, and in a low voice that Hannah had to strain to hear, he told her that the girl's name was Vera. Her parents owned a parcel of land on the other side of the creek from the Alstadt's land. She had told Sewell that she would like to see him again at the next church meeting. He had promised Vera that he would try to be there the next time but it would depend on if he got all the farm work done in time. Hannah was delighted to hear that bit of news because it meant that she might be able to go with him, if she got her chores all done as well.

Chapter seven

Hannah and Sewell continued to make regular trips to church and into town for Saturday night parties. They were confident that their parents did not realize that they were talking with other people in the community as they filled the wagon with supplies or that they were attending church on a regular basis.

Sewell was courting Vera on a regular basis. He would sometimes sneak away at night after his parents were in their usual fighting routine after they had gone to bed. Sometimes the parents were so noisy in their verbal fighting that anyone could have slipped out of the house unnoticed.

Hannah had not managed to be bold enough to slip out of the house at night, but she had been spending a lot of time talking to one of the young men at church. His name was Bartell. He had told her that he had a small piece of land over behind their farm on the other side of the woods that separated them. His owning a piece of land all his own impressed Hannah. He had also told her that he had a team of mules that he used to farm the land, and a dairy cow that he used for milk. Hannah allowed her better judgment to soak it all in, believing every word that he uttered.

Bartell also told Hannah that she was the most beautiful girl at the church. He loved her auburn hair, he said, and he wanted to take out the braids and touch her hair to his face.

Hannah never felt beautiful. She was sure that she was just plain. She did not have pretty ribbons for her hair or fancy hats to shade her face. She knew that each spring she would have a new crop of freckles sprinkled all over her face and arms. In addition, she still had not learned how to take one of her mother's dresses and cut it down to fit her small frame. She knew that she was developing a stunning shape under all the volume of fabric but she did not understand how she could make her waist appear tiny or her breasts look voluptuous while her body was still wrapped in her mother's clothes. However, she watched all the other girls at church to see what they were wearing. Maybe she could figure out a way to make her clothes look like theirs.

Bartell continued to cozy up to her at every opportunity that presented itself. Most of the winter had passed before Hannah could manage to be at church or in town more than three times. Her mother would not let her venture into town with Sewell. She would demand that Hannah do more work at the house, or she would send her to the barn to help her father and brother, saying that there was work to be done. No young girl should go gallivanting into town or church when she was needed to work at home, her mother always said. Hannah accepted the restrictions with disappointment, but she was confident that when the spring thaw came, she would be allowed to go to church again.

Chapter eight

Hannah was right when she thought spring would bring more opportunities to get out of the house and away from her parents. She was even more thrilled to see that Bartell was still interested in being her friend. He continued to seek her out at the church meetings and at the socials held in the town square. She often wondered how he would suddenly appear each time she was in the area. Nevertheless, she wanted to spend time with him so she failed to notice that he was also attentive to some of the other girls too.

Bartell seemed to be enamored by Hannah. He saw her as a stepping-stone in his life. He knew that she was a strong woman and would be a good helpmate for him to work on the farm. He also had other thoughts about Hannah. He was sure that she would be a beautiful woman when she removed all her clothing. He could only envision what their 'love life' would be. He had been raised on a farm and saw the animals mating before his eyes. He longed to have a wife with whom he could mate as he had seen the farm animals do.

Chapter nine

Bartell and Hannah continued to see each other as often as possible. Hannah had just turned 16 years old, and she was sure that she was all grown up. Bartell had told her that he was 17 years old and that he was a man. He began to try to become 'familiar' with Hannah. He wanted to feel her breasts. He wanted her to show him her stockinged legs. Then he asked her to remove her stockings so that he might see her bare legs. Hannah was not aware that these were not customary requests that young men made of any girl. She assumed that every man treated his girlfriend that way. She was slow to allow him to see her legs without her stockings but when he continued to touch her breasts she began to think that perhaps it was the right thing to do. She noticed that he only wanted to do these things when they were behind the church or in the woods behind her house. However, Hannah enjoyed the attention that Bartell was giving her so she rationalized it as accepted behavior.

One day, when she was in the barn with Sewell, she asked him if he had ever seen Vera's legs without her stockings on them. Sewell was aghast. No gentleman would ever ask a lady to do such a thing before they were married, he replied. He would not dream of dishonoring Vera by asking her to remove her stockings unless they were man and wife. Hannah recoiled at the statement that her brother had just made. She was not about to tell Sewell what had been going on with Bartell. She preferred to keep her secret to herself. Now there was a big dilemma. Should she tell Sewell that Bartell had been fondling her breasts? If she told him that, Sewell might rise up against him and do bodily harm to him. Worse yet, if Sewell confronted Bartell he might not ever come around Hannah again and she would not have a beau. She hardly knew what to do.

Hannah waited until the next Saturday party in town and then she decided that she would confront Bartell about him being too 'familiar' with her. He took her behind the general store to talk to her and before she could say anything to him about his behavior, he grabbed her in his arms and began kissing her on the mouth. Hannah was in shock. She hardly knew how to react but she was sure that it was not a proper thing to do. She pulled away from his grasp and began smoothing down her dress, which he had managed to pull up to her waist. "I don't think you should do that, Bartell," she said.

"Oh, you know how much you like it," he replied. "I can see your eyes light up when I touch you." "You are an eager young lady."

Hannah did not know what he meant by her being an eager young lady, but she did admit to herself that she had a strange feeling in her stomach when he kissed her.

Bartell slowed down his actions and began to smooth her breasts with his hands, and then he kissed her neck as he slowly massaged her lower back. Gradually he lowered his hand to fondling her derriere. As he was using his left hand to caress her buttocks, he was using his right hand to fondle her breasts. Soon he had her dress unbuttoned and his hand was inside on her bare skin. Hannah did not know what to do. She was sure this was wrong, but she was helpless to stop him. She now realized the strength of his hands and arms around her. She was held captive. He quickly wrestled her to the ground and pulled her dress up above her head. As he continued to kiss her on the lips, he pulled down her drawers, and, as quick as a wink, he penetrated her. Hannah wanted to cry out in pain, but he held his hand over her mouth preventing her from screaming. It was only a few strokes of his heavy body on her and he fell off her. He continued to hold his hand over her mouth to prevent her screaming. He gathered his wits about him and proceeded to explain to her that she was now his 'woman'.

Hannah looked at her rumpled clothing and saw that there was blood on them. She was horrified. She was afraid to go home. She knew that she would not be able to hide this from her mother. She was frightened of what Sewell would do to him when she shared her experience with him. In addition, what would her father do?

Bartell helped her to her feet and held her in his arms. "You are my beautiful woman," he said to her. "If we can meet again, I will teach you even more," he continued. "You need to learn a lot more about the art of being a woman."

Hannah glanced into his eyes and wondered what else there was to learn because this had not been a very pleasant experience. In fact, it hurt a lot. She was not sure she wanted to learn any more of those lessons.

Chapter ten

Sewell and Hannah headed for home after the Saturday night party. They rode in silence for a short distance with only the 'clop, clopping' of the mule' hooves. Suddenly, Hannah could hold her secret no longer. She tried to explain to her brother what had just happened to her. She was not sure what his reaction would be but she wanted to ask him what to do.

Sewell was shocked that Hannah had been so violated by a man that he thought was a friend. He glanced over at Hannah and asked her what she wanted to do. "You have been raped, unless you gave him permission to do this," he said.

"I did not know what he was doing, Sewell." "I've never had this happen before. No one has ever told me what to expect from a man. Did our father ever tell you what to do to a woman?"

Sewell thought about her words. No, no one had ever explained anything to him either, but he was aware of what the fighting was about in the bedroom of their parents. However, he had seen the animals mate and no doubt Hannah had not witnessed any of these activities because her mother always kept her inside. Sewell realized just how naive Hannah was and at the same time, she was so vulnerable to someone as brutish as Bartell.

When the two reached their house, the light was still on in the kitchen. Sewell went in the door first and stated that he and Hannah had something to tell their parents. He quickly spilled out the story about what had happened behind the general store. Hannah's mother became hysterical. She demanded that the man be brought before them. He should also be punished. Hannah's father, on the other hand, was quite calm and cool. He calmly questioned Hannah about her actions. Had she encouraged the young man to molest her? Did she return his favors? Was she willing to allow him to get under her clothing? And, what did she do when he had finished with the dastardly deed?

Hannah trembled as she relived the events of the last two hours. "I didn't know what he as doing," she replied. He kissed me on the neck, and I thought it was nice. He asked to see my stockinged legs and I showed him. Then, he just kinda took over from there and threw me to the ground. It all happened very fast, Daddy." With the last statement, Hannah began to sob. Her mother rose to comfort her daughter. She was smoothing her braids as she picked the straw and dirt from her hair. She noticed that her dress was soiled and then she noticed the spots of blood on it.

"There's no use, Dad, she has been violated." "He must marry her as soon as possible," she stated rather succinctly. "He will not be allowed to do this to the other girls in the community. Hannah will become his bride".

Chapter eleven

Hannah Alstadt became the bride of Bartell Hauptman on the following Sunday. The ceremony was held in the church where the two of them had been attending. No one in the Alstadt family ever mentioned anything about the events that happened behind the general store just a week before. They were interested in preserving the good name of their daughter rather than any punishment for the groom. Bartell took Hannah over to his house to live just behind the woods that separated his house from her parents.

Chapter twelve

He had told Hannah that he had a small farm and a house. Hannah winced when she saw his house. It was very little more than a hog shed. The floors were dirt. The walls were open to the wind and weather. It was only one room and it was totally empty. There was a pile of straw and a blanket in one corner where Bartell had been sleeping. An old wooden crate stood on end in the center of the room and it appeared that he ate his meals from there. There was no fireplace but a large iron pot on the side of the room. From all indications, he would build a fire in the pot, and then cook over the open flames. There was no need to worry about any smoke accumulating in the room since the cracks in the walls was adequate ventilation.

Hannah leaned against the door and tried hard to conceal her disappointment. In fact, she tried to hide her disgust. How could she live like this? She could not hide her feelings or the urge to run through the woods back home.

Bartell sensed her discomfort and began to try to explain that he had been living there alone since he had run away from his parent's home. He tried to tell her that he would help her make it a better place to live. He stepped over to her and put his arms around her to try to console her, he was immediately aroused. He quickly threw her down on the straw pile; pulled her clothes up and raped her again.

Hannah realized that this probably was the way it was going to be in the 'hog shed' and she would need to be prepared for these sudden outbursts.

Bartell nestled in beside her and began to tell her that he was so in love with her. He wanted to be more patient with her but she was such a beauty that he found it hard to go slowly.

Hannah began to realize that she was becoming a 'grown-up' in a very short time. She was thinking about many things that maybe she would ask her mother, if she ever saw her again.

She got up off the straw mat, smoothed her dress and looked around the room to see where he might keep anything to eat. It would soon be suppertime She was convinced that she was expected to cook him a meal.

Chapter thirteen

Hannah tried hard to settle into the 'hog shed' the best way that she knew how. She managed to find an old broom out in the lean-to barn. She perused the barn and tried to convince herself that the 'hog shed' was better than the barn, but it was sure a close contest. There were some big boards in the barn, and she dragged them into the house to try to make a worktable. She found some more boxes like the one that Bartell had been using for a table and she brought them inside. She could stack them on top of one another and make places to store her supplies. She also found an iron rod that she could put across the iron kettle to use as a hanger for smaller pots to cook over the coals.

Bartell was not completely oblivious of the efforts that Hannah had made to make the 'hog shed' a better place to live. He even praised her for all the changes that she was making.

Bartell made a trip into Griffin and brought home flour, sugar, beans, and some lard. He showed her where the root cellar was out behind the 'hog shed' and took her to the well, which was about 300 yards away.

After Hannah had spent the day trying to get the hog shed cleaned up and ready to live in, she wondered what to do about the bed. It appeared that Bartell did not need any other kind of bed. He was certainly making good use of the one that he had.

Early one afternoon, she began to try to figure out what she could cook for them to eat. She found some turnips and carrots that had been grown the previous season. She put a pot of beans on over the hot coals and decided she would drop some turnips in the cooking broth near the end of their cooking time.

It was not a bad day for Hannah. She had a place to live, a place to cook, and a place to sleep. In addition, she had a man who loved her or at least lusted for her. What more could she want?

Chapter fourteen

Hannah and Bartell managed to make a home out of the 'hog shed'. She mastered cooking over the open iron pot. She gathered eggs from the hens; she milked the cow, and she cooked their meals. She carried in the water from the well and scrubbed his clothes on the rocks that stuck out of the ground behind the well. Keeping the floors of the house clean was not hard. They were dirt to begin with, so she only had to sweep them lightly to clean up the surface dirt.

Bartell worked the fields with the mules from sun-up until sundown. He assured Hannah that they would have a crop this year, if the rains came as they usually did. He plowed a garden spot with the mules and showed Hannah how to plant a garden for vegetables in the summer.

As busy as she was, she noticed that she was beginning to get bigger around the waist. She did not think that she was eating more than usual, so she wondered why she was getting fat. She only had two dresses that she had brought with her from her mother's house and they were becoming too tight. She started wearing the shirts that Bartell had hanging on the peg near the bed.

Bartell was very observant. He noticed that she was becoming a bit fatter around the middle. He was not sure what the problem was, but he was certain that he did not want his wife to get fat and lazy. He needed her to work in the fields with him. Hannah had become quite accomplished at driving the mule team. He wanted her to do the plowing while he tended to the other farm chores or spent time clearing the land behind the house of stumps. He needed more land to grow more crops. He also continued taking his weekly trips to town.

BARTELL

Chapter fifteen

Bartell Hauptman was born into a very poor family in 1831. His family had migrated across the Anderson River into rural Perry County, Indiana. They were without any place to stay so his father had built a lean-to against the rocky hillside and the family remained there for several years. Times were hard for the family. Bartell's father worked in the farm fields for other farmers in the area. His pay was usually some of the food that was grown on the farm, a few eggs, a bucket of milk, or what he could forage from the neighbor's gardens. His father was stealthy and could make off with two days vegetables before the owner knew anyone was outside in the yard.

Bartell was born during the second year that his family lived in Indiana. He was not a welcomed sight since the family barely had enough to feed themselves. His father considered him just another mouth to feed and too small to be of any help on anyone's farm. His mother was deprived of enough food to even give Bartell much milk to suckle and the boy grew to be skinny and sickly from birth. He had a large head full of bright auburn hair and seemed to be all arms and legs. As Bartell began to grow in age, his father was extremely cruel to him. He considered his son a burden and constantly ridiculed him because of his stature and lack of stamina. Bartell wanted to find some comfort in the arms of his mother, but she was so intimidated by his father that she only cowered in fright when he spoke. She tried to shield her son from the wrath of his father, but she did not have the courage to confront the older man.

Bartell was beaten and abused repeatedly as a young boy. His father used any object as a weapon that was within reach when he thought his son did not respond to his commands as quickly as he should. He demanded that the boy do work with the mules that were well beyond the small child's ability. When Bartell failed to meet his father's demands, the father beat him mercilessly. Bartell began to fear being within earshot of his father and tried to hide from him. This only brought on more wrath from his father and the beatings would resume.

Bartell had no opportunity to get away from the hillside hut until he was nearly 12 years old. By the time he had reached his twelfth birthday, the boy was frightened and bitter in the face of any authority. He soon realized that he had no ally in his mother who was just as afraid of his father as he was. She, too, was the victim of his father's abuse. Bartell witnessed his mother's severe beatings at the hands of his father as well, and she seemed helpless to stop the abuse.

One morning, shortly after the spring thaw, Bartell gathered a gunnysack and raided the kitchen of the hillside hut. He took biscuits, potatoes, eggs, and a few dried beans that he stuffed in his sack. He headed off toward the west, having no idea where he would go or how he would live. He only knew that he could live better without the beatings that he had endured at the hands of his evil father.

Bartell roamed the hills of Southern Indiana for many months. He had learned, early on, how to raid a neighbor's garden or hen house at the hands of his father. He had no weapons with which to hunt game, but he knew how to take a long stick and make a fishing pole. He could catch fish and sometimes had to eat them raw. He lived by his wits in a very god-forsaken countryside.

One evening, just after the sun had gone down behind the hill, he happened upon a man riding a horse. He saw that the man had a rifle strapped to the horse. He flagged the man down and asked him for a ride. The kindly neighbor gladly hoisted Bartell up behind him on the horse; he also asked him where he was going. The stranger mentioned that he had not seen Bartell before. Bartell mumbled something that was probably not heard or understood by the stranger. As they traveled down the dirt road toward the stranger's home, Bartell had an idea. He took his neckerchief from around his own neck and quickly looped it around the neck of the stranger. He tightened it so quickly the man was unable to fend off the vicious attack. The stranger soon fell into unconsciousness and slid off the horse. Bartell took the reins and galloped on down the road to wherever the path would take him.

Bartell had tasted his first bite of freedom. He had a horse and a gun. He knew nothing about either of them, but he had the necessary tools to help take care of himself. He was free at last even though he had taken a man's life to get there.

BACK TO GRIFFIN

Chapter sixteen

Bartell knew that his wife was probably pregnant. He knew that when the farm animals mated, the females always got that way. He did not like the idea, but he knew that it was bound to happen. His idea of a wife was one that he could sleep with on the straw tick and would also work in the field. Hannah was a good wife. She had taken the hog shed and made it into a decent place to live. She worked in the field with him on most days except for the times that she prepared their food to eat. If she really was pregnant, she would not be able to work for about 3 months; one month before the birth and two months after the birth. If the baby lived, it would need care for the young years of its life. Bartell did not like the idea of a child being under his feet as it was growing into an age when it might work on the farm. However, the die was cast. He could do little about it now.

Hannah did not know much about having a baby. Her mother had never discussed any of these types of things with Hannah. Since her brother was older than she was, there was never an occasion for her to learn. When her breasts became tender to the touch, she was alarmed at what the problem might be. Soon, she was feeling nauseous in the early morning. Finally, Bartell told her that she was going to have a baby. Hannah was delighted. She was sure that the baby would be something that she could love and cherish. In addition, perhaps Bartell would not be so cruel to her if there was a baby in the family. She tried even harder to satisfy Bartell's every demand so that he would not beat her so often. She also was afraid that in one of his fits of anger, he would do something to harm the unborn child. However, she was wrong about the beatings diminishing. In fact, he seemed to be angry more often than usual. So, the beatings continued in a regular pattern.

Chapter seventeen

In the spring of 1851, Hannah gave birth to a baby boy. Bartell attended the birthing and cut the umbilical cord. Hannah had insisted that he go for her mother, but he refused. He assured her that he had birthed many cows in his lifetime and he knew how to handle a human baby. The baby survived his untrained handling and crude methods of his birth, a birth which Hannah was certain was a God given miracle. They named the baby John. Hannah was able to suckle the baby early so that he did not cry much. She was afraid if the baby cried, Bartell would harm him.

As soon as Hannah was able to stand on her feet, she strapped the baby in a sling around her shoulders and went to the field to work with Bartell. They had a crop to put out and animals to tend, so there was no time to waste on recovery time.

John was a good baby. He never seemed to mind the fact that his early life was spent in a sling or that his meals were skimpy since his mother did not have the right kind of food for herself.

Baby John was growing like a weed. Hannah

would take him to the fields with her and tie him to a fence post while she tended to the planting. Before he could walk, John had spent most of his life in the field near the team of mules as his parents struggled to plant a harvest for their own survival.

Hannah longed to visit her family, to tell them that she had a baby grandson for them, but Bartell forbad her to leave the house. He was afraid that if she ever left him, she would not return. Often her face was covered in bruises and gashes from his treatment, and any exposure to the outside world would bring down the wrath of the townspeople on him.

Chapter eighteen

When John turned one year old, Hannah realized that she was pregnant again. Bartell was very angry that she would be having another child to take care of. Hannah was afraid to mention the pregnancy until she began to show and Bartell recognized the symptoms. He flew into a rage and the result was a severe beating that she had not had for quite some time. He particularly tried to strike her where he thought it would cause her to miscarry the baby. However, this baby was tenacious and it hung onto life in its mother's womb. Hannah continued working in the fields while Bartell was trying to clear more land to plant. He spent his days chopping the brush that had grown up on the north side of his land. He swore that he would have an additional acre of tillable land before the next spring. The winter storms had kept him out of the field for a large portion of the season, but in spite of the bitter cold, he had almost accomplished his goal.

Chapter nineteen

It was nearing the end of the year, and Hannah realized it was nearly time to deliver this new baby. She was so cumbersome that she could hardly get around the small house. John was almost 18 months old. He had been walking about six months so she did not have to carry him. She considered that a small blessing.

Weather had turned bitter cold and keeping a fire going in the iron pot to heat the house was a big chore. Bartell had chopped enough wood to burn, but she worried about how to keep a new baby warm. She hoped there would be a break in the weather before the birthing was to take place. Again, she begged Bartell to go for her mother, but he refused using the same argument about his ability to birth a child.

In the early morning hours sometime in middle December, Hannah began to experience labor pains. She kept quiet about her condition until she was sure that the birth would be soon. By daylight, she knew the time was here. She awakened Bartell and told him that the birth would be within the hour.

He hurriedly stoked up the fire and put water on to heat, knowing that he would need it to help with the birth of this baby, too.

Hannah did not seem to have a difficult time with this birth, perhaps because it was not her first. Bartell pulled the baby free and cut the umbilical cord. He wrapped the baby in a clean rag and started to hand the crying newborn to its mother. Suddenly, he noticed that the baby was a girl. He began to rant and rave that baby girls were worth nothing on the farm. He did not want a baby girl. He wanted boys who would grow up to be farmers and help raise crops or clear land or breed animals. A girl was worth nothing to him.

Instantly, he grabbed the baby from Hannah's arms and began to choke the baby. Hannah raised her body from the straw tick and began to scream that he should give her the baby. She was begging him to give her to its mother. She began to cry and scream for her child. He paid not attention to Hannah. He continued to choke the baby until the crying stopped and its body went limp. Hannah threw herself at him and threatened him with all her might, but it did not matter. He walked to the box by the iron pot and put the body of the baby in the wood box. Hannah knew that he would throw it in the fire if he had a chance.

With the blood from the birth running down her legs, she put on her boots and heavy coat and retrieved the body of her baby from the wood box. She wrapped it tightly in the birthing rags and carried it around until Bartell went to the barn to tend to the cows.

As soon as he was out of her eyesight, she quietly slipped out behind the house and managed to dig a hole in the backyard under a big oak tree. Hannah pulled back the rag that was wrapping the baby and peeked at the small lifeless body. The child had a fair complexion and long silky eyelashes. She could hardly hold back the tears as she slipped the baby's lifeless body in the hole and covered it over with the earth. She place a large chunk of wood over the burial spot hoping that the wild animals would not disturb the grave until the ground was thawed enough to dig a proper burial place. She decided to name the baby, Sara.

She went back into the house and fell almost lifelessly into the straw tick; her energy was spent. She could hardly believe what had just happened to her. She had given birth and buried her little baby girl all in the same day. As she fell asleep, she could only think about how her life might have been if she had never met Bartell. Hopefully, tomorrow would be better for Hannah.

Chapter twenty

Spring came early in Griffin, Indiana in 1852. The flowering trees in the woods south of the Hog Shed began to blossom. The maples and the oaks began to bud out and Hannah knew that it would soon be time to plant the vegetable garden. She enjoyed that part of farm life. She loved to watch the plants take root and come peeking through the dirt.

She had carefully dug a better grave for baby Sara while Bartell was in town one Saturday. She marked the grave with a cross that she had made from two old slats of wood. She would use berries to mark the name on the cross when fall came and there were elderberries on bushes near the edge of the woods. She could see the grave from her tiny window in the 'hog shed'. She cried for the baby who never had a chance. At the same time, she shuddered when she thought about a man who was so ruthless as to snuff the life out of a tiny helpless child. Hannah was not certain, that if he were angry enough with her, that he would not snuff the life out of her as he had done Sara.

Her son John was two years old. He was not big enough to work on the farm, but he followed his father around as he went to the barn to tend the animals. Soon, Bartell had taught him how to gather the eggs that the hens laid on the ground in the barn. John was proud to be able to work for his father. He quickly learned to stay out of his shadow or his father would smack him in the face. Hannah cringed when she saw the handprints on little John's face, but she knew the wrath of the man who systematically beat her for almost no reason, and knew that he could mete out unwarranted punishment to a small child.

Hannah longed to visit her parents or hoped that they would visit her. However, Bartell forbad her to cross through the woods to her father's farm, or to take the wagon into town. He knew that if she visited them she would tell the tales of the awful life that she was living. He also feared that she would tell them the story of Baby Sara. So, visitation was forbidden at any time.

Hannah asked to visit the church where they had met, but Bartell refused her the right to go to church, also. Hannah would like to take John and show him to her friends, but it had been so long since she had seen any of them, they were probably not in the community any longer. She resigned herself to being content in the Hog Shed, with her son, John, and their meager farm.

Chapter twenty-one

In the summer of 1853, as Hannah worked the vegetable garden, she realized that she was pregnant again. She dreaded telling Bartell of her condition because of his dislike for more children. She also worried that she might have another girl. She could still see the look on his face as he squeezed the life out of Sara. She wondered what would happen this time. Nevertheless, it was inevitable that he would realize her condition soon. She began to plan when she thought the birth might be. She figured that it would be sometime in early February of 1854.

The Hauptman family made it through the winter of 1853. The garden had been quite successful although Hannah was very uncomfortable as she worked in the garden. She seemed to grow bigger every day. When Bartell discovered that she was pregnant again, he was adamant that she continue to work as usual in the fields as well as the family garden. His hope was that somehow her work would affect the baby and force a miscarriage. He did not want more children. Nevertheless, neither did he intend to forego any of his sexual activity with his wife. She was his property and he continued to make use of her as often as he could.

It was January in 1854, when Hannah took to the straw tick to deliver her third child. As usual, Bartell was to be her midwife. Again, she begged him to go for her mother to assist him, but he would not hear of it. He reminded her again that he was quite skilled at this job, since he had successfully delivered the other two babies. However, he was in for a great surprise this time.

Hannah delivered her second son and he was a healthy looking baby. A surprise came when Bartell realized that there was another baby inside. Hannah had not even considered that she might have twins. She had almost no knowledge of any bloodlines in her family and even less about Bartell's family. A set of twins only complicated her life, she thought. For her to deliver twins was a complete shock. However, when the babies were both born, Bartell was happy to know that they were both boys. Hannah breathed a sigh of relief when she realized that neither of the babies was a girl. The twins were plump and healthy at birth. She judged that they each weighed about five pound at birth. They each had a tuft of bright red hair on the top of their head and rosy cheeks making them look like cherubs.

Bartell seemed a bit more pleased with these babies than he had been with John. He never showed much interest in him, but these two seemed to steal his fancy. He would occasionally cuddle the two as if he had done it all alone. Hannah was surprised at his reaction, but she was too exhausted to care, and she slipped off to sleep often while he was discovering the joys of fatherhood.

Bartell would place the babies by her side and after a short nap, she would begin to nurse them. The two babies eating from her took all her strength and before long, she realized that she must begin eating again. She smiled when she realized that the summer had been a good time for growing things, and there was plenty of food in the root cellar. Even though John was only four years old, he could retrieve food from the root cellar and assist Hannah in preparing something to eat for the whole family.

Chapter twenty-two

The family continued to work the fields, tend the cows, pigs, and chickens. Bartell had purchased two more young pigs from a farmer in Griffin. He was convinced that they could raise hogs and butcher them for additional meat. The two cows gave them milk for the table and Bartell sold some of it in town to the local grocer. He was also able to sell eggs to the same merchant. With this additional money, he found things to spend it on when he made his trips into Griffin. They needed more space for the babies, whom they had named Mark and Luke. Hannah remembered those names from the Bible lessons that she had heard in their church which she attended so long ago. It seemed like years since she had been allowed to go to church.

On one of his trips into Griffin, Bartell brought Hannah a bolt of fabric, needle and thread and a pair of scissors. He wanted her to make herself a dress. She had worn his shirts or her old dresses until they were just a pile of rags. Now, she could make herself something to wear. He stated that he was weary of seeing her in rags.

After the birth of the twins, Bartell did not seem to be as angry about everything. The beatings subsided for a short time. He continued to be cruel to John, expecting more from him than a small child could do. If Hannah tried to complain about his treatment, Bartell would take his frustrations out on her. She wondered if the twins would be the one thing that softened the demeanor of their father. She often wondered what effect the beatings that she endured would have on the children, since he never seemed to care if they witnessed his cruelty or not. Sometimes she watched as John cowered in the corner when his father was administering his almost daily beatings to her. When he could get away, he would run to the barn and hide until he was certain that it was safe to return. John always came to her aid when he could avoid his father's wrath.

Chapter twenty-three

By 1860, Hannah and Bartell had made a decent life for themselves and their sons. They still lived in the Hog Shed under very cramped quarters. Hannah could never bring herself to refer to it as a house. The large iron pot was still their only heat and cooking fire. She also heated water on the fire to wash their clothes. She would wash them outside in the yard when the weather permitted and spread them on the fence around the front yard.

The twins were six years old and able to do many things on the farm. They had learned to milk the cows, gather the eggs, work in the garden, and help to store things in the root cellar.

Hannah watched as her family continued to grow. The boys were gregarious and loved to be outdoors. It was not wise for them to play too far from their house. Bartell had told her that the woods behind the house were filled with wild animals. He had seen wolves and bears roaming there. They heard wolves howling in the night. Bartell knew that if the animals were hungry, they would attack small children. Hannah tried to keep an eye on the boys when they were in the fields working or when they were playing in the yard by the barn. The thought of them straying to the woods was terrifying to her.

Bartell was not a very good hunter. Although he still had the rifle that he had stolen from the rider on the horse, he was not a very good shot. If he was going to shoot something, it had to be rather large. Rabbits and squirrels were usually safe from the bullets in his gun. However, he had in mind that he might get a bear for them to use. A bearskin cover for their bed would be great to warm them in the winter. The bear would provide meat for them and the fat from a bear could be used as oil for a lamp. It would also burn in the iron pot to add additional heat when the weather turned extremely cold.

Hannah did not favor the idea of trying to dress a bear. She did not know how to clean one and she was sure that if Bartell shot one, she would have to clean it.

If he was going bear hunting, she certainly hoped that he would get a small one, and that he was able to kill it before it killed him.

As luck would have it, on Bartell's second trip to the woods on a bear-hunting excursion, he came home with a bear. Although it was not completely dead, he had fired three shots into its charging body.

He managed to wound it badly enough that it was immobilized. Bartell was able to drag the bear home and proudly show it off to the family. To assure himself that the bear was dead, he took an axe to its head and bashed it in mercilessly. Hannah cringed at his cruelty, but then she realized how cruel it would be to let it suffer. The thought crossed her mind that he could probably kill anything and not have a guilty conscience. He had proven that to her.

The family all participated in dressing the bear. John was not much for killing animals, so he was a reluctant helper. However, the twins were into it as much as six year olds could be. Mark relished the idea of a bearskin on his bed and he wanted to go hunting with his father the next time. He was sure that he could get a bear and make a cover for Luke's bed too.

In time, Bartell taught the boys how to shoot although his eyesight did not seem to be as keen as theirs. Mark took to the gun like a duck to water, although the gun was longer than he was tall. Luke was anxious to learn to shoot but he much preferred to dig in the dirt. It appeared that he might become a good farmer of the land. Bartell was glad for the help in plowing and tending to the planting. John was not interested in any of their hunting expeditions. He would rather be at home with his mother, helping her in the house or the barn.

On the rare times when Bartell would take the boys to town, they loved riding in the wagon with the mules. They enjoyed the sights that they saw in Griffin. They saw a few people who had horse-drawn wagons. When the boys saw a carriage, it was a real mystery to them. They questioned their father as to who would own such a fine piece of equipment. Bartell assured them that the local banker probably owned it. That was a surprise to them. They did not seem to understand why anyone would want such a fragile piece of equipment or even who a banker might be. They only had one horse, he was old, and only used for riding. A team of horses drawing a wagon or a carriage looked like a rich man's life to them.

The newspapers that John saw posted around town fascinated him. He asked his father if he could have a newspaper to take home. Bartell felt that he could not read it, so there was no need to pay a penny for one. The shopkeeper went to the back room and brought out two papers that were several days old and gave them to John. He was delighted. He convinced himself that he could learn to read them on his own. Those old newspapers became his very own possessions. He would guard them with his life.

While they were in town one day, a man came up to Bartell and began to talk to him. He asked about Hannah. He wanted to know how she was doing. The boys did not know who the man was, but their father told the man that she was fine and healthy. Bartell never mentioned that the boys were her sons. He simply got in the wagon and headed for home.

John could hardly wait to tell his mother that an old man had asked about her. Bartell quickly stopped the child from saying any thing more about the older man. John took his days old newspapers and disappeared into the barn.

Hannah knew it was her father who had asked about her. Within herself, she vowed that someday soon she would see her family again.

Chapter twenty-four

Hannah continued to handle the day-to-day operations of the family. The boys were becoming more grown up and the work piled on them by their father was overwhelming. Bartell seemed to think that the twins could plow with the mules although they were under 10 years old. John was approaching 12 years old and he could cope with his role as a farmer. He was tending to the animals and working the fields as he was instructed, and hiding in the barn to read when he had the opportunity.

One day, in mid-afternoon, a group of four uniformed riders rode into the yard. Bartell was in the barn, but when he heard the horses and saw the men, he came to the house to see what they could possibly need from him or his family. The men dismounted and began to talk to Bartell. Hannah heard the commotion and came to the doorway to see who was making the noise. She could hear the men talking, but she was not sure what their intentions were for her family. She wondered where the boys were and if she needed to protect them. She listened to them talking for a few more minutes and decided that the soldiers were friendly folk. She turned and went back to preparing their evening meal.

After talking with the riders for only a few minutes, Bartell came into the house to tell Hannah that he was joining the Union Army. The riders were with the 154th Regiment of the Indiana Volunteers. They promised him a gun, a pair of shoes, and a uniform. He would be taking the horse but would not need his clothes or his gun. He would go to Fort Benjamin Harrison somewhere near Indianapolis and eventually fight in the Civil War with Grant's Army. Hannah had little or no idea about the Civil War or Indianapolis.

She could hardly grasp all the things that Bartell was telling her. She only watched as he gathered his personal belongings and went to the barn to get the horse. One of the riders stepped up to her to tell her that her husband was going to be a soldier in the War Between the States. They would make sure that he would return to her safely when the war was over.

In less than 15 minutes, Bartell mounted the old horse and rode away. Hannah was not to see him again for many years.

Chapter twenty-five

Hannah settled in to be a mother to her three sons. Although Bartell had taken the horse, he had left her with the gun. She was sure that the gun was more valuable than the horse, since she would need the rifle to defend themselves against the wild animals in this wilderness. She was not sure that she was sorry that Bartell was gone. She knew that she would need to do the work that he had done when he was there. However, she also realized that he had not done much around the farm lately, so her work would not multiply in his absence.

She gathered the boys around her and tried to explain to them what had just happened. She repeated to them the words from the rider who had assured her that her husband would return to her when the War was over. John spoke up and said that he had been reading about the War. The newspapers called it the Civil War.

Hannah was surprised that John had been able to teach himself to read. What a blessing it was for him to be able to tell her what was happening in the world outside of the farm.

Chapter twenty-six

The day following Bartell's departure, Hannah gathered the boys around her and asked them to harness the mules. They were going to take a trip to town, and then on to visit their grandparents. Hannah could hardly wait to visit her mother and father. It had been more than 12 years since she had been allowed to visit them. She had been held captive in the Hog Shed by Bartell. Suddenly, she felt liberated. She was convinced that the boys could work without being beaten to do so.

As the family rumbled across the covered bridge over the creek, Hannah remembered how fascinated she had been with the swirling water below. She asked Mark to stop the wagon so that she could look down and watch the water. She still wondered where the water went as it hurried downstream. Nevertheless, more than anything, she knew that she felt as free as the water, at least as long as Bartell was gone.

Following their trip into town, they headed for her father's farm. When they pulled into the yard of the small house where she had grown up as a child,

Hannah fairly flew out of the wagon and ran up the walk to see her family. When she burst through the door, followed by three young boys, it nearly scared her mother out of her wits. She and her parents were hugging and crying and trying to talk all at the same time.

The boys were startled to see such a display of affection. They had never seen anyone hug each other. Bartell had never talked to the boys; he only beat them when they did not do as he expected them to do. Bartell had not ever talked to their mother; only beat her when she did not meet his expectations. His anger often manifested itself during a meal, or at bedtime, or at sunrise. His actions were always unexpected and cruel.

Hannah tried to tell her mother and father about the last 12 years in short sentences. Then she realized that the bad part of her life did not need to be told. She, then, began to tell about how the boys were growing and about their talents. She bragged on how John had taught himself to read by sounding out the words that he saw in old newspapers. She talked about what a crack shot Mark had become and that he had managed to shoot a bear out in the woods behind their house. Then she told them that Luke could plant a garden and harvest enough vegetables to feed them all winter.

Hannah's mother and father were astounded at what had happened to their beautiful daughter in the last few years. Her father tried to get Hannah to tell him just what Bartell had been doing all these years, but she only said that he worked the farm, and hunted for wild game in the woods behind the house.

Mr. Alstadt did not seem to accept that response very well, but he assumed that he would learn more about the lives of his family in the coming months.

Hannah's mother came to her side and began to ask about how she had delivered the babies all alone. She could hardly believe that Bartell had helped her deliver her babies without outside help. Her mother silently surmised that Hannah had been one lucky girl, not to have lost her children with such archaic methods of childbirth.

As the afternoon wore on, the stories of farming, living in the Hog Shed, the soldiers, and Bartell's absence seemed to flow like water under the old bridge. Hannah left out most negative things, and John seemed to understand that he should not tell his grandfather that his father had mistreated his mother so badly. He silently kept the information to himself. John knew that someday he would be free to tell them of the real stories that occurred in the Hog Shed.

Hannah began to question her mother about where Sewell was. If he had been working in the barn, he would have noticed that a strange wagon had pulled into the yard.

Mrs. Alstadt tearfully announced that the same soldiers came to their house too. She stated that Sewell had ridden away with them and joined the army too. Sewell had seemed anxious to go fight the war. He had been very interested in Grant's Army, and he was convinced that he could help win the battles. However, Mrs. Alstadt did not share his enthusiasm and she felt that Sewell would never come home except in a pine box. Hannah had loved her brother very much and she hoped that her mother's prediction would not be true.

The afternoon wore on and Hannah knew that she and her sons needed to get home to tend to the animals. Suddenly, Mark and Luke began to talk about the Hog Shed. They questioned their grandparents about how they could make their house as nice as theirs.

Mr. Alstadt turned to Hannah and asked if, in fact, they were living in a hog shed. Hannah dropped her head and confessed that their living conditions were horrible. She stated that Bartell had never allowed her the opportunity to do much to the old building. He insisted that the cattle deserved the better place to live since they were sustenance for the family.

As Hannah was loading up her sons in the wagon, her father came over to her and stated that he would see her the next day. He intended to help her, if he could.

Chapter twenty-seven

When morning came at the Hog Shed, true to their word, Mr. and Mrs. Alstadt paid a visit to their daughter's humble home. Her father was shocked to see how his baby girl had been living. He assured her that he and her boys would assist in closing up the cracks in the walls to make the building warmer. He also wanted to build another room on the side of the building so that the boys could have a better place to sleep. He thought that perhaps they should put a floor in the 'house' so that their beds were not lying on the dirt floor. He thought that maybe, if the boys could bring enough stones from the fields, they could put in a fireplace for heating and cooking. The old iron pot needed to be moved outside.

Hannah's mother came with some of her clothing that she wanted to give to her daughter. They talked of making some new things for her.

In addition, Mrs. Alstadt noticed that the boys clothing was almost threadbare. She wanted to help make them some new things too. Hannah could hardly believe how kind her parents were to her after all the years that she had been gone. She wondered how she could ever repay them for their generosity. She was very unaccustomed to anyone being kind to her. Suddenly, she realized that she had hardly noticed that Bartell was gone. She had not missed him at all. For the first time in years, she could sleep at night without being sexually assaulted or beaten. In addition, she noticed that the boys were sleeping quietly too. John no longer escaped to the barn to get away from the conflicts that went on in the Hog Shed.

Chapter twenty-eight

Work on the 'house' began immediately. Mr. Alstadt arrived with lumber and tools. He also brought with him a hound dog for the boys. When he stopped in town to pick up the lumber, a man at the lumberyard asked if his grandsons had a dog. Mr. Alstadt stated that he was sure that they did not have one. The old man said that a stray had wandered into the back lot a week or so ago and no one had claimed him. If Mr. Alstadt wanted to take the dog for the boys, it was to be a gift to them. He loaded the dog in the wagon and headed on down the road to present the boys with their gift.

When the grandparents arrived at the Hog Shed to begin work, the dog jumped out and greeted the boys with licks and a wagging tail. It was a sight to behold. Three boys and a happy dog were all yelling and barking at one time. The boys had never had the opportunity to have a pet because their father would not allow it. His complaint was that the dog would eat too much food that the family needed.

After a short time, Mr. Alstadt urged the boys to help him unload the wagon and begin the work on their house. The dog was going to stay for a long time, and they could play with him later. They named him Shep. Hannah felt sure that it was a good name for a dog who would be the shepherd over her boys.

The boys jumped in to help their grandfather do what they could, although they were still children. Their grandfather was shocked to see how capable they were for their ages.

Hannah and her mother were busy trying to keep the working crew fed. They also were actively trying to improve the wardrobe of the entire family. Life was suddenly so peaceful for all of them.

In just a few days, Hannah discovered that she was probably pregnant again. Bartell was gone, but apparently he had left his 'deposit' inside of her just before he left, and he would not know that she would have another baby in his absence. She smiled when she realized that this baby would be delivered by her mother and not by him.

Hannah shared her news with her mother and the two of them danced around the room where all the men were working to try to make the Hog Shed into a home. Of course, the men hardly knew how to react to the news. Her sons only laughed at the prospect of have a new baby in the family. However, this time, the boys seemed happy to hear the news.

A dog and a new baby seemed to be the news of the day.

Just before the sun began to fade, the workers stopped for the day. Mr. & Mrs. Alstadt left for home and vowed to come back soon to finish their task of helping their baby daughter make a Hog Shed into a decent home for her family.

Chapter twenty-nine

Winter was fast approaching in Griffin, Indiana. The weather was usually a mix of snow and cold wind. This year, Hannah had a home without cracks in the walls. She had a fireplace to keep herself and her sons warm. She could hang a pot to cook her food over the coals in the fireplace and make a decent meal for them. They had tended the farm well and had a good stock of food in the root cellar. The young pigs were grown and would be ready to butcher by early spring. Everything seemed to be going fine. Bartell had not been heard from since the day he rode off on the old horse. Hannah was not sorry. She dreaded the day that he might return, but she knew that she was still married to him. So if he came back, she would have to be his wife.

The impending birth of her last child would be sometime around Christmas. She did not want it to be born when it was time to butcher the pig. She wanted her baby to be old enough and she wanted to be well enough to assist in the butchering. She was sure the boys could not handle this job alone.

One night, in late fall, she heard the dog barking in the dark. She looked at the old clock on the wall and saw that it was nearly 2:00 A.M. She could not imagine what the problem was outside, but she was afraid that a wolf or even a bear was in her yard trying to get at her livestock. She did not have more than she needed for her family's needs, so she knew that she had to find out what the problem was.

She calmly went to John's bedside, awakened him, and stated that there was something or someone in the yard. He heard the dog barking and believed that his mother was correct. Something or someone was outside. John pulled on his pants and started to go with Hannah to survey the situation outside. He stopped at the door and said, "Mother, I am not the one to go with you outside." "If this is an animal, we might need to shoot it. I do not know how to shoot the gun. We need to wake Mark. He can shoot to kill whatever it might be." Hannah, smiled at her son, and agreed with him. The dog had seemed to stop his barking. While Mark was getting dressed, Hannah looked out the side window of their room. She could see a figure in the barnyard. She was even more frightened than before. What if it were Bartell? What if it were soldiers? Was it someone trying to steal her pigs or her chickens? All of these questions ran through her mind in an instant.

Mark took the gun down from the wall and

walked cautiously with his mother by his side into the barnyard. When he got to a safe distance from the figure, he yelled, "Stop or I'll shoot." No doubt, the figure realized that this was a child yelling for him to stop, but it was evident by the size of the gun, that the voice meant business.

"Please don' shoot, missa, I means no harm," the voice answered. "I needs a place to sleep til mornin' and then I'd be a moseyin on." "This here dog and I dun made friens, and he likes me."

Mark lowered the gun and looked up at his mother for instructions. "Put the gun away, Mark." "He isn't going to harm us."

Hannah walked up to the black man and saw, by the light of the moon, that the man was just a boy himself. She walked over to him and asked what he wanted from them. He told her that he had run away from a cruel master in Tennessee. He was trying to get up North before someone caught him and returned him to his master. He only wanted to sleep in the barn. He kept telling her that the dog had welcomed him. As he was talking, the dog was wagging his tail and licking him the same way that he did the boys.

Hannah placed her hand on the young man's arm and told him that she would get him blankets so that he could sleep comfortably in the barn and not freeze on such a cold night. She invited him to have breakfast the next morning. They would talk at that time. The man placed his long boney fingers on her hand and thanked her for her kindness. Hannah knew instantly that this young man had been a farm worker somewhere by the calluses on his hands and the strength in his arms. Nevertheless, he appeared to be hungry. She sensed that he had not eaten for several days.

Mark, John, and Hannah went back into the house and prepared to go back to bed. Luke had not awakened and did not have any knowledge of the happenings. John lingered by his mother, as she was getting ready to get in her bed. "If he is a worker, why not let him stay? We could use a hard worker on the farm. He would not eat much; no more than my dad did, and he would be a strong helper for Luke" John said.

"We will see what morning brings, John. If he is a strong worker, then maybe you are right, we should let him stay. Luke has slept through all this, so we will need to catch him up on all the details in the morning. For tonight, let's try to get some sleep," Hannah said, as she hugged her oldest son while urging him to go back to bed.

Chapter thirty

When morning came, the snow was blowing and the temperature had dropped considerably. It was almost blizzard conditions outside. Hannah was up and had a breakfast of eggs, potatoes, meat, and coffee ready when the boys awoke. She sent John out to the barn to find their guest. It had snowed so much during the early morning hours that the path to the barn was almost obscured from view. In a few minutes, John returned with the young black man trailing behind him.

The family gathered around the table and began to eat. The black man hesitated to join them in the meal. Hannah assured him that he had her permission to eat with them. "I ain' never et with white folks before," he said. "I allus had to take my plate to th outside."

"You may eat at our table, young man, just as anyone else would. Tell me, what is your name and where did you come from when you wandered into our barnyard?"

"My name is Taylor, ma'am and I come from down Tennessee way." "I'se been tole that the

president done freed the slaves, and I wanna be free."
"I ain got no kinfolks, they dun gone th other way."
"I figured I could find me someplace up north."

Hannah looked the young man over again in the light of day. He was obviously accustomed to hard work. John was right. They could sure use another hired hand on the farm. "How old are you, Taylor?" she asked. "I'm seventeen, I think, ma'am, but I don knows for sure." "But, I can work like a man."

The boys looked from Taylor to their mother to see her reaction. Luke had no knowledge of who he was or where the man came from. However, he knew that Taylor was a welcome sight on the farm, and they all knew he would not be beating them with a stick as their father had done.

"We don't have much money to pay you, Taylor, but if you want to stay with us, you can eat with us." "We need help on the farm, and the boys could sure use your help in the fields." "I think it is too cold for you to sleep out in the barn tonight, so you can make a bed in the room where the boys sleep." "Right now, I think we need to see what we need to do before this blizzard hits us any harder."

Taylor jumped up from his seat and shook Hannah's hand. He pumped her hand hard to show his appreciation for this opportunity. In a flash, the boys were wrapped in their heaviest coats and started out the door. They turned around and noticed that Taylor had no coat. Hannah walked over to the peg on the wall and gave him Bartell's coat. He shook her hand again. Hannah smiled at the gratitude of a young man to whom she had given so little and yet it was more than he had ever had.

The boys tied a rope to the back door and walked through the high drifting snow to the barn. They tied the other end of the rope to the barn door. If the snow got too deep or the wind blew too hard for them to see, they could follow the rope back to the house. As the boys threw down hay for the cows and fed the chickens, Taylor began to draw water for the animals. He knew that the water would freeze by morning. In addition, he would need to draw more water the next day. However, Taylor knew that the animals still needed water to survive in the bitter cold weather.

They all finished their chores and started back to the house. As they figured, the blizzard was blowing so hard they could hardly see the house. Taylor had been living in the South, so he was not accustomed to this kind of weather. He willingly followed the boys as they held onto the rope to guide them back to the house. Once inside, he began to shiver from the cold air. Hannah instantly brought him a cup of hot coffee to warm him inside. She wrapped the bearskin cover around him and sat him before the fireplace until he could get warm again.

The weather continued to get worse before the next morning. Hannah put on a big pot of soup to feed them for the next couple of days. There was not much to do inside until the storm broke. They began to tell stories about things that happened in their youth. Taylor told about being on his 'massa's' farm. He told about working in cotton fields and hoeing cotton with a short hoe. He told about being whipped when he did not seem to be working fast enough for the boss. John, Mark, and Luke did not say much, but it was obvious that they had endured much the same treatment as this black man sitting in their room. Their beatings came from their father, and they were not slaves. It seemed strange to them that they had been treated the same way that the slaves of the South had been treated.

Chapter thirty-one

It was three days before the weather let up so that the boys and Taylor could get out of the house. They hurried to the barn to see if the livestock had made it through the blizzard without freezing to death.

The chickens seemed to be fine but welcomed a drink of water. One of the pigs had wandered out of the lean-to that was covered, and could not find its way back. They boys found its body in the corner of the lot. The cows and the mules seemed to be fine, but they looked a little hungry. It took most of the morning to fill the water trough again, and feed them more hay. Taylor mentioned to the boys that he was sure learning a lot about how to live in the North.

Hannah had not mentioned to the boys that she was going to have another baby. She was not sure how they would take the news, but it was obvious that she would deliver sometime in the early spring. She wanted to make sure the boys and Taylor would know how to go for her mother when her labor pains began. At lunchtime, she told them that she had some good news. They were all ears to hear what it might be.

"I am going to have another baby," she said, quietly. Taylor was not surprised. He stated that he noticed that she looked 'in a family way', but he did not want to mention it. "My momma had lots of babies," he said. I ain' de oldes, I had a sister older dan me, but I am the oldes boy. I helped my momma birth the last two babies, cause my sisters were working for the 'massa'," he continued. Hannah breathed a sigh of relief. If the boys could not get to her mother in time, Taylor knew how to birth a baby. John, Mark, and Luke began to babble about a new baby. It had been several years since there had been a baby in the house. "What would dad say about this baby?" John asked.

"He is gone, John, and we will welcome this baby into the home, just like I did Mark and Luke," Hannah replied. "You better hope it is a girl so that you will not have to do the housework," she continued. Hannah's body shook when she realized what had happened to her last baby girl. She had mixed emotions about what this baby might be. If it were a boy, he would have to work like the others, and if it were a girl, she would raise her to be adored by her brothers. When Bartell returned, Hannah hoped she would be old enough that her father would not strangle her. Her thoughts of Sara brought tears to her eyes. She glanced out the window to the hillside where she had hastily buried her baby daughter and wondered what she would be like if she had lived.

When lunch was finished, the boys went to the field with Taylor to show him around their farm. Mark took the gun, hoping to see something he could bring home for the evening meal. Taylor knew nothing about hunting for animals, so he was eager to see Mark shoot something. As they traipsed through the woods looking for game, Luke spotted a bear. It was a small bear, but big enough to make a cover for his bed. He quietly pointed out the young bear to Mark. The brave hunter stalked the bear until they caught the animal out in a clearing. Mark raised the long rifle and took aim at the bear. He knew that he would have only one good shot to bring the bear down. He also knew that if he missed with his only shot the animal might charge him and his brothers. Mark was a calm hunter although he was very young to be hunting on his own.

The gun went off with a loud bang and the boys waited to see if the shot from Mark's gun had been successful. The bear fell and began to moan, and roll around. Mark waited to see if the bear was going to die or if he would need to re-load and shoot it again. John mentioned that the mother of the bear might be nearby and would charge the boys. John did not like hunting for animals. He thought it was almost barbarian to shoot an innocent animal. In addition, he was concerned that the mother bear would be nearby. He did not like the choices, so he announced that he was going home. He turned and left the hunting party and began to run toward the house.

Mark, Luke, and Taylor crept slowly toward their bounty. If the bear were dead, the three boys would try to drag the bear back to the house. The other alternative was that Mark could re-load the gun and shoot it at close range to finish the job. As the boys got nearer to the animal, the thrashing had stopped and the bear was completely still. Mark's shot had hit the bear right behind its right ear. It had lived only a few minutes. Mark was very excited to think that he had managed to kill his first bear, they would have fresh meat for the next few days, and he would have a great bearskin cover for his bed next winter.

Hannah met the boys at the door when they came home with their prize. Her concern was that she would have to clean the dead animal. However, Mark, Luke, and Taylor assured her that they could do the job. She agreed to let them try. She would assist them if they needed her. Suddenly she realized that John was not among them. She asked the others where John was and why he was not with them. They mentioned that he did not want to watch them kill the animal so he left for home. Perhaps he was in the barn reading his latest stack of newspapers. Hannah hurried to the barn to see if she could find him. When she went inside the barn, it was obvious that he was not reading the newspapers. He had packed the papers neatly in a wooden box with a rock on top of them.

Hannah went into the house to see if she could find him; however, he was not inside either. She went back to the boys and insisted that they help her look for him. Mark managed to get the bear carcass inside the edge of the barn away from any animals, and joined Luke and Taylor to look for John.

Hannah was eight months pregnant so she was unable to do much walking or climbing over branches in the woods. She remained at the edge of the woods, and waited for the boys to report to her on any sighting of their brother. The boys searched through the woods for several hours. Hannah was very worried and very tired. She wanted to help them but she was not able. Finally, she returned to the house to rest. She prayed. She was not sure that she knew how to pray, but she remembered the preacher at the church saying that anyone could talk to God. As she sat at the table with a cup of coffee, trying to build up her strength, she began to talk to God. She begged him not to take her oldest son. He had been her rock during her struggles with Bartell. She knew that he was not the same kind of person that his father had shown himself to be. John hated violence and he would have escaped, if he had ever had the opportunity.

When it began to get dark, Hannah wondered why the boys had not come home. She went back to the woods and began to call for them. When she listened for their answer, she heard Mark answer her. "We are here, mother," he said. "We are coming home. We have John's body," he said.

Hannah nearly fainted when she heard these words. Did he mean that John was dead? What seemed like hours, but in reality was just a few minutes, Mark, Luke, and Taylor emerged from the woods, carrying the bloodied body of John. Luke spoke first and stated that apparently a bear had mauled him. John would have been helpless to fend off any bear. Mark felt that the bear mauled John in retribution for the death of her cub. Mark began to weep as they tried to explain why their brother was so savagely killed. "I never meant to bring harm to John," he cried. "He was my brother. He wanted to teach me to read and write," he continued. "I am so sorry, Mother, for bringing him harm."

"It is not your fault, Mark; perhaps the bear was hungry." Hannah did not want Mark to carry the guilt of this tragedy and she continued to console him. She, herself, was grief stricken. She had asked God to save her son. Now she felt betrayed by the only source of power that she had. As the group walked back to the house in silence, each one of them had thoughts on their mind.

Luke wanted to tell John that he had wanted to learn to read. He yearned for John's ability to remain calm in all times of calamities. John was their strength during the blizzard. He really wanted to tell John how much he meant to him. However, there was no time. Luke just hung his head in silence as they carried the body to the house.

Mark was filled with guilt. If he had not killed the baby bear, maybe the mother would not have killed his brother. He wanted to tell John how sorry he was for all of the pain he had endured. He wanted to tell him not to be afraid in the dark. He wanted to say that he would gladly let John use the bearskin cover when it was cold. However, he never got the chance to tell him any of those thoughts.

Taylor hardly knew John. He was convinced that John would have taught him to read, too. He knew that John was smart and would have grown up to be a fine man. John would never have to work in the fields or be beaten by his 'massa' again.

Hannah spread food on the table for the family while the men were in the barn cleaning the bear. She was so heartbroken that she could not eat. She knew she would need to send the boys over to her parent's house to tell them that their oldest grandson was dead.

She decided that she would send them in the morning. Tonight, they laid John's body in the back room and covered his body with an old blanket. The boys did not want to sleep in that room tonight so they brought their covers into the kitchen and slept in front of the fireplace.

Hannah could not sleep. After she was sure the others were asleep, she silently crept to John's side and began to talk to him. She thanked him for protecting her from Bartell when he could. She told him how much she had loved him. She whispered that she would put him beside Sara to sleep forever. He was the only one who knew about the hideous death of Sara. Now John and Sara would sleep side by side forever. They were her firstborn children. She drew back the cloth from his face and wanted to kiss his forehead. However, his face was so badly mutilated that she covered it again and mumbled to herself that she would remember his beautiful face as she had seen it the day he was born.

Hannah stumbled back to her bed and fell into a deep sleep until morning.

Chapter thirty-two

Early the next morning, the boys awoke and slipped out of the house to tend to their chores. They had cleaned up most of the mess of the bear from the night before, but now they needed to prepare the meat for cooking. They had lowered the carcass into the well for safe keeping the night before. Taylor milked the cows, and fed the pigs. He scattered grain for the chickens and looked for eggs for their breakfast. While he was doing the work in the barn, Mark and Luke had cut up the meat and had it ready to take inside the house.

Hannah finally awakened to find the boys outside doing their chores. She cooked something for them to eat and called them in for their morning meal. As soon as they had finished eating their breakfast, she announced that Mark and Luke should go to her parents' house and tell them the news. She and Taylor would prepare the ground to bury John. Taylor spoke up to say that he had helped to bury children that his mother lost. Hannah assured him that she hoped they never had to bury anyone else in her family.

The twins harnessed the mules and attached the wagon to the doubletree. They went off toward town to their grandparents' home. Hannah marked off the place next to Sara where they would bury John. It would take a bigger grave to bury Sara's brother than she had dug to bury Sara. Taylor wanted to know about Sara, but he was afraid to ask. He took his long bony finger and traced the letters on her grave marker. His eyes questioned the grave.

"She was my baby daughter," Hannah said. "She died when she was a baby," she continued. She left off the part that her father had murdered her. That was a secret that only she and John knew which he now had taken to his grave with him.

"My momma los some of her babies, too," Taylor said. "She jus bury dem in da back yard, lak you do," he said. "She don know what else to do." "She jus sings songs an cries loud."

"I have heard you singing in the fields as you are working. Do you know some songs that you can sing at John's grave, Taylor?"

"Yasum, I knows some of de ones dat my momma sings."

"Would you sing a song for my John?" Hannah asks. "He would like for you to sing to him. Then, I would feel like he has had a Christian burial".

"Ah kin do dat, ma'am, if you want me to."

"I think that John would like that, Taylor."

When they had finished digging the grave, they went to the barn to look for wood to make a cross. Taylor climbed up high and took a piece of wood from the corner of the roof. He took the wire and wired a cross together. Hannah mentioned that they would have to wait until fall to get elderberries to make ink to put his name on the cross, but Taylor said he would find a walnut shell to use. He wandered around out in the back of the barn and came back with a handful of walnuts. He took a brick and smashed them to get the greenish brown stain to mark the cross. Hannah watched the skilled hands of this young man and knew that this was not the first grave marker that he had ever made.

When the boys returned, her parents were right behind them in their wagon. Her father wanted to know all the gory details of the accident. Mark stepped up to his grandfather and said, "I told you all the details when I was at your house. I do not want my mother to relive the accident all over again." With that remark, Mark took Luke by the hand and they went to the hillside where Hannah and Taylor had prepared the grave for John.

Mark, Luke and Taylor stood side by side at

the grave of their brother. Hannah knelt at the foot of the grave. Her parents stood on the other side. Hannah announced that Taylor would sing a song that he sang at his brother's funeral. The family was astounded. They had no idea that he could sing.

"Swing low, sweet chariot, comin' fo to carry me home," Swing low, sweet chariot, comin' fo to carry me home."

"I look over Jordan, and wha do ah see? Comin fo to carry me home, a band of angels comin after me, comin fo to carry me home."

Taylor paused and looked to Hannah for her acceptance. She smiled and asked him to sing another song. She loved his melodic voice. He seemed to be giving his best to honor John.

"Go, down, Moses, way down to Egypt lan. Tell ol Pharoh, let my people go." "This boy don need no Pharoh, he don ben released."

Taylor sang two more verses as the family stood in awe of the talent of this young man. When he finished his singing, he wiped his eyes, and knelt by the grave and said a few words that no one heard.

The parents went inside with Hannah as the boys filled in the grave and put the cross at the head. No one asked about Sara. And Hannah never spoke her name.

Chapter thirty-three

It would be Sunday on the next day, and Hannah announced that they would all go to church on Sunday morning. She wanted her sons to learn the same lessons that she had learned in church so many years ago. Taylor knew about church. He had attended church in the community where he lived. He was not sure that he could go to church with Hannah and the boys. She assured him that he could and would go with them into town and to church. He might be expected to sit in the back, but she was sure that he would be welcomed.

Early in the morning, they finished their breakfast and brought the wagon around to the front of the house for the trip to town. Hannah was excited to go to church again, and she wanted to see her old friends; she wanted to hear 'church' music; she wanted to hear the preacher deliver a good message.

Hannah also wanted to learn more about how she could cope with the death of her son. She thought she could get some guidance on how to raise her other sons so that they would not be in any more danger.

As the wagon rumbled across the covered bridge, she noticed that the water in the creek was high and it was running very fast downstream. The mules ambled on across the old bridge and carried their cargo to the church.

When Hannah went inside, the preacher came to welcome her. He remembered her from her youth. He had been in the same group of young people that attended the parties on the square in Griffin. He spoke to her about the black boy who would have to wait outside.

"No," she said. "If he must go outside, then I will join him. He is my helper on the farm, and I will not make him stand outside. He can sit in the back row, if that pleases you, but if he can not worship in this church, neither will my family," Hannah stated. The preacher seemed shocked at her response. He had never had anyone question his rules before, especially a woman. He was not sure what the congregation would say if he allowed a black man inside the building.

Hannah turned to walk out the door with her sons, when the preacher took her by the arm. "You may stay, Mrs. Hauptman, and the black man may sit on the back row," he said. Hannah went to Taylor and showed him where he should sit. Then she took Mark and Luke by the hand and led them to a seat near the front. When the congregation rose to sing the hymns, she noticed that Taylor sang with them. He knew songs that she had never heard before. She wished she had known more about church before she reached this age, but she was determined that she would learn as much as she possibly could now.

Chapter thirty-four

In the fullness of time, the weather had improved, and it was time to begin preparing the land for planting. Taylor was so strong and knew a lot about planting, even though his planting experience had been with raising cotton. He knew how to use the team of mules to plow the fields. He also knew how to plant crops in rows so that the rain would be absorbed into the rows and not run off the land.

One Monday morning, while Mark, Luke and Taylor were busy in the field, Hannah knew that it was time to deliver her baby. She wanted to wait until they all came in for lunch, but she was not sure that this latest child would wait that long. She prepared the necessary rags and hot water that she would need for the birth. In addition, she prepared their lunch and had it ready on the table. She knew that there would not be time to get her mother. She smiled when she realized that she had begged Bartell to get her mother each time that she delivered a baby. This time, she was not afraid to have it alone, and she did not think that she needed her mother. After all, this was her fourth child, and she had got up off the birthing bed to bury Sara. She knew that she was strong enough to do this with the help of Taylor.

When the boys came in for lunch, they found their mother in her bed in the throes of delivery. She had been having labor pains since shortly after breakfast. Now was the delivery time. Mark and Luke were astounded and did not know what to do. They were hardly old enough to understand childbirth. Taylor told them to step out of the room and he would take over. Hannah accommodated him and had about three more strong labor pains. Suddenly she delivered a baby. Taylor cut the umbilical cord, cleaned up the baby and announced that the boys had a baby sister. He carefully wrapped the baby in a clean cloth and gave it to its mother. Hannah was quite pleased that the baby was a girl; she cuddled it next to her and began to try to make her eat. She smiled at her sons and told them to think of a name for their sister, as she slowly slipped off to sleep. It was the spring of 1862.

Chapter thirty-five

The Hauptman family named the baby girl, Lydia. She would grow up to be the darling of the family. She had a cherubic face and a head full of dark auburn hair. She was a 'toy' for Mark and Luke who carried her everywhere they went unless Hannah forbade them to take her. They made a cart from some scrap lumber and harnessed it to the dog. The dog seemed to understand the task that he had been given: to give the baby Lydia a ride around the yard of the house. As the boys watched their pet work to make sure that the baby had a good trip, they cheered and clapped their hands to cheer the dog on. Hannah watched her family play and laugh, something they had not been able to do for several years.

Hannah sent the twins over to her mother's house to announce the news. When they returned, Mark announced that his grandmother was not doing well. She was in bed and unable to join them in the living room. Their grandfather was trying to take care of her and the farm at the same time. The two boys assured him that they would return and help with the spring plowing.

In just a few short weeks, Hannah would make a trip to visit her mother and take Lydia with her. She intended for her mother to see her newest grandchild.

The weather was turning warmer, and it would soon be time to start their rigorous plowing and planting of their land. Taylor had cleaned a bigger spot for their vegetable garden and the twins would have it ready to plant soon. They had carefully made boxes to start the tomato and sweet potato plants. Their 'starts' were nearly ready to be put in the ground.

Early one morning, Hannah took Luke with her to handle the wagon and the mules as she visited her mother. She carefully dressed the baby in a new dress that she had made for her, and wrapped her in a new quilt. It was the baby's first trip away from the security of her home. The trip was also an opportunity for Hannah to get out of the confines of the house. She and the baby were expecting to have a good trip.

Just as the boys had reported earlier, her mother was not well. She was quite frail and could hardly talk to Hannah. Her voice was faint. She seemed ghostly white and weak. Hannah did not know what to do but she tried to feed her some broth. Her mother could only swallow a few spoons full. Hannah went to the other room and spoke to her father about the health of her mother. He did not know what kind of an illness that she had. He had summoned the doctor from Griffin but he only mentioned that it was "a sickness unto death". Hannah was appalled that her father simply was waiting for her mother to die. She returned to her mother's bedside and whispered that she would be back soon to visit with her.

Hannah wrapped her baby daughter in her quilt and asked Luke to take them home. She rode in silence as the mule team took them toward home. When they crossed the old bridge, Hannah glanced down at the swirling water and wondered if the water ever stopped anywhere.

Three days later, Hannah prepared some soup, some of her homemade jam, and a loaf of fresh bread to take to her mother. As she and Mark were getting ready to leave, her father appeared, riding on his horse as fast as he could.

"Come quickly," he said. "I think your mother is dying. She doesn't seem to be breathing."

He turned his horse around and headed back toward his house as Mark and Hannah came behind him in the wagon.

When Hannah arrived at the house, she rushed in to see if she could help her mother. It was too late. Hannah knelt beside her mother and tried to rouse her from her sleep. However, when Hannah reached out to touch her mother, she saw that her skin was cold and slightly blue. Hannah laid her head on her mother's breast and cried tears for the woman who had given birth to her. She wanted to say one more time, how much she loved her, but it was too late.

Hannah slowly rose to her feet and faced her father. "I want to bury her at the church cemetery," she said. "I think my mother would like that."

"She never went to church, Hannah. Why would she want to be buried there? I'll put her up on the hillside."

"No, Dad, I want to bury her at the church. She often told me that she wanted to go to church but the work always had to be done. It was you, Dad, who would not go to church, not my mother."

Her father turned to go out the door, but paused and said, "Do what you like; she is your mother."

Chapter thirty-six

Mark and Hannah headed for home with a heavy heart. As they passed the chapel, Hannah asked Mark to stop. She climbed down out of the wagon and went inside the church building. She went to the front of the church intending to pray for her mother. When the pastor came out of his study, he greeted Hannah and asked if he could help her.

"My mother just died," she said. "I would like to bury her here if it is ok. She was not able to come to services much, but she wanted to be buried in the church cemetery."

The pastor walked to Hannah's side and put his arm around her shoulders in an effort to comfort her. Her first instinct was to pull away, but it seemed so nice to have a man touch her who was not going to hit her that she turned and looked into his face and smiled.

"Of course, she can be buried here. There will be no charge for the burial, but someone will need to dig the grave," he said.

"My sons will dig the grave," Hannah said. "I will have my hired hand assist them," she continued.

"Can we do this tomorrow? You will provide some words at the funeral, won't you?"

The pastor smiled at her again, and stated that he would handle all the arrangements if she could have the grave opened. The service will be in the afternoon, he stated. "That will give your sons and Taylor time to get everything ready."

Hannah was filled with excitement and sadness at the same time. She had lost her mother, but it seemed that she might have a friend in the pastor.

Hannah and Mark hurried home to their house. Mark and Luke headed back to their grandfather's house to tell him that all the arrangements had been made to bury their grandmother. They took Taylor with them. They stopped by the church to meet with the preacher to see where they needed to dig the grave.

Chapter thirty-seven

The funeral service was held the next afternoon. The boys and Taylor had finished their job of digging the grave in time to attend the service. Several of the people from the church were present at the funeral. Although many of them did not know the deceased very well, they came to the service because she was Hannah's mother. Taylor had made a cross with her name on it for the grave.

SARAH ALSTADT
1804-1863

Hannah clung to her father as she cried tears of sorrow for her mother and for all the times that she needed her but was not allowed to ask for her help because of Bartell.

When the service was over, the pastor came to Hannah and again expressed his sympathy. He asked if she would be in church on Sunday. "Oh, yes, Hannah replied, I wouldn't miss it."

Hannah and her family quietly left the church yard and rode in the wagon toward home. No one spoke a word as they traveled down the narrow dirt road. Hannah had many thoughts running through her mind. The pastor was so kind to her. She could only imagine what being with a man who was kind would be like. She smiled when she thought about him, then shamed herself for having such evil thoughts on the day they had buried her mother.

The next day Hannah traveled to her father's house to see if there were things that he wanted her to take home with her. While she was there, visiting with him, a man came on horseback, into the yard. He was in a Union Army Uniform. He came to the door and before he could knock, her father opened the door to greet him.

"Are you the father of Sewell Alstadt?" He asked.

"I am," her father replied.

The soldier handed him a piece of paper, then he stated that Sewell had been killed in the battle of Gettysburg.

Hannah went to her father and tried to comfort him. She wondered what he would do. His only son was gone, and he had just buried his wife. She led her father to a chair on the front porch. She turned to the soldier and asked, "do you have his body?"

The soldier looked at her and hung his head. "No, ma'am, we do not have a body. I only have his duty papers. The body was left in the field at

Gettysburg. Someone there might have taken him to a mass burial site. I am so sorry for your loss." The soldier turned and walked back to his horse and mounted it. He galloped back onto the road and out of her sight.

Hannah thought about the times that Bartell would not let her visit her family. Now she had no adult male except her father. It seemed so unfair. She vowed to herself that she would never allow her sons to be so cruel to anyone. She would try to be both mother and father to them as long as she was able. She wanted them to grow into fine young men who had respect for everyone. Right now she needed them to help her take care of her father.

Chapter thirty-eight

Spring merged into summer. The crops were good and the rains came as if on schedule. Taylor announced that if nothing bad happened they would have a bumper crop of corn and wheat to sell to the mill in Griffin. Mark and Luke went to her father's farm and helped him get in his crop as well. Her father seemed to have adjusted well to the loss of his wife and his son, Sewell. He seemed to be cooking for himself and enjoying the food that Hannah sent over to his house with the boys. His health seemed strong and he was able to tend to the animals on his farm.

Hannah and her family attended the church in town each Sunday. She listened intently to what the pastor was saying. He seemed to be speaking directly to her although she was sure that it applied to the entire congregation as well.

At the end of August, the church was planning a 'dinner on the grounds' event. It was a picnic and the women of the church would cook their special foods. A large wagon would be brought to the churchyard and the food would be spread on the wagon. In the afternoon, the men and boys of the church would play softball or pitch horseshoes for entertainment. The women would sit in the shade and talk about what was happening in the community.

When August came, Hannah enjoyed much of the picnic. She had very little time otherwise, to visit with her neighbors. The children all played in the yard all around the church. Hannah kept her eye on Lydia since several of the women wanted to hold the baby.

The pastor seemed to be paying some attention to Hannah, but she did not want to think about him. He surely knew that she had a husband in the war somewhere, and that she had three children.

The preacher came to her side and asked her if she wanted her children to be enrolled in the school that was just down the road from the church. Hannah wanted them to go to school, but she was not sure if she could spare them from the farm. She wondered if Taylor would be able to handle all the chores that the boys could not get done before they left for school. Hannah looked into the preacher's eyes and stated that she certainly wanted them to be educated. She would discuss it with them and report to him whatever their decision might be on the following Sunday.

BACK TO BARTELL

Chapter thirty-nine

When Bartell had ridden off with the soldiers that had come to the farm, he was riding the same horse that he had stolen from the man near Tell City. The horse was old, but was able to carry its rider on his way to join the army. The soldiers told him that they were all headed to Fort Benjamin Harrison in the middle of the state of Indiana. Bartell would be sworn in at the fort and issued a gun, a new horse, a uniform, and a new pair of shoes. He smiled at his good fortune. He had not had a new pair of shoes in several years.

Once the soldiers were outfitted, they were ordered to go to Tennessee to the battleground at Shiloh in order to fight off the Rebels there. Bartell hardly knew what the War was all about. He could not read the newspaper and had seldom listened to the townspeople in Griffin when they had talked about the War. However, he was a willing soldier because it seemed like an easier job than trying to eke out a living on a piece of ground in Posey County.

He was convinced that fighting along side a band of soldiers was better than raising a house full of kids. Needless to say, he was about to be surprised.

The company of volunteers traveled by train from Indiana to Savannah, Tennessee, under the command of a Lieutenant Sullivan. He would lead them to the Tennessee River where they would board a boat or barge to go to Pittsburg landing at the base of the hill of Shiloh.

When Bartell arrived at the battlefront, he found that there were sixteen thousand Indiana troops prepared to fight for the Union Cause. As they went up the hill to confront the Rebels they were ordered to go to the right. Bartell hesitated only a few seconds and decided that he did not like this environment. He quickly fled to the left. He hurried up the hill and into the woods where he stayed hidden while the smoke of the gunfire and cannons filled his nostrils. The battle lasted two days and Bartell could not believe the carnage that he saw. The battlefield covered acres and acres. The battlefield was littered with dead bodies. He could not find even one of his buddies still alive after such a horrendous battle. Their regimental commander gathered the remnants of his Indiana Volunteers together and they were reassigned to the Regular Union Army, then they were dispersed into other battles across the southern edge of the War. Bartell had rejoined them as they were re-grouping.

Bartell had certainly seen more of the war than he had ever intended to see; however, there was no going back. It was soon discovered that his eyesight was not very keen and that shooting was not his best ability. His commander decided that he make a good cook. He was assigned to the 'mess tent' to prepare meals for the soldiers. Bartell could handle his duties as a cook. He would also wander off to forage food from the nearby farmer's garden or chicken house.

He plundered farms and fields as they moved through the countryside. Bartell loved that part of his job. He was very good at finding farms with growing crops where he could steal potatoes or corn for the evening meal. He could catch chickens or a goose for cooking in the blink of an eye.

Bartell hardly thought about the life he had left in Griffin. He only missed romping in the straw tick that he had enjoyed with Hannah. However, he knew that many of his antics in the straw tick had produced more children, and they were the bane of his existence.

As the troops moved from battlefield to

battlefield, some of the farms had been burned to keep the enemy from reaping any benefits from the farmers' efforts. Bartell's foraging began to become more difficult as they fanned out to each new battle.

The troops were forced to hold farmers and their families' hostage while they ransacked the farm home. Often the summer kitchen would be a building in the back of the house. Bartell would raid the kitchen while the other soldiers raided the interior of the house.

Once, and then often, Bartell joined them in the house, and was surprised to find a lovely woman inside. He realized how easy it was to take her to her bedroom and 'take' her on her elegantly covered bed, an experience he had never had before now. Admittedly he enjoyed that experience more than his romps on the straw tick. His brutality was the same. If she did not submit to him willingly, he simply strong-armed her into submission and finished his dastardly deed in record time.

As the War continued, Bartell was sent all over the northern part of the country in search of food and spoils for the 'Cause'. He was never forced to march in line with soldiers or carry a rifle or shoot a Rebel during his time as a soldier, but he carried a pistol that he had taken from a Rebel soldier for his own protection, However, his ruddy demeanor intimidated a lot of 'folk' along the way. He had a scraggly red beard and a huge head full of auburn hair. He was rarely clean and usually was odiferous from several paces away. He was completely unconcerned about his persona and continued to pursue the scavenging that he so enjoyed. Bartell was a man "unto himself".

Chapter forty

In 1865, the war ended after 4 ½ years of fighting. Lee surrendered to Grant at Appomattox virtually ending the war. Lincoln had signed the Emancipation Proclamation earlier setting all the slaves held by landowners in the South free. Many of the freed slaves began their trek North in search of a better life. All of these events had little or no influence on Bartell. He considered himself free from all encumbrances including a wife and sons that he had left back in Griffin.

When he was notified of the war's end, it only meant that he did not have to answer to any commander. He could still wander the country and live as he pleased. He had a horse, a pistol, and a decent outfit of clothing. He simply continued pillaging throughout several areas in the eastern United States.

Bartell had been gone from Griffin for more than four years when the war ended. In his mind, he was not sure that he would ever want to go back there. He could only remember how grubby poor he had been when he lived there. He considered the life that he was living now, a lot better than what he had experienced before.

He began to roam from town to town. Many of the Constables or local Sheriffs took a dim view of anyone who continued to wear his Union Army uniform and carouse around their towns. Bartell discovered that he was not welcome in areas where he hoped to buy a hot meal. His response was to 'hit the road' again with Army issued horse. He wandered throughout the North until the winter winds began to blow, and then he decided that he would go south where it would be warmer. If he were forced to sleep under a bridge, at least it would not be in the snow.

Bartell was quickly becoming a Renegade. The countryside was full of them. However, he soon found that to be successful in the South he had to shed his uniform. He wandered upon a Rebel soldier on his way home, and he promptly overpowered him and took his uniform, leaving him his Union uniform in exchange. He found that the uniform was his passport into many communities. However, when he tried to pillage a southern plantation, they thought he was an errant Rebel and he was met with a lot of resistance.

Bartell soon found that his best line of action

was to raid the plantation owner's homes and take what he was able to carry. He often found that he could take their silver or jewels and sell them for money. He had never had much money in his life, so this was a lucrative "job" for him. He also found that the beautiful women on these plantations were easy prey to satisfy his insatiable appetite for sex.

Bartell was enjoying the life that he was living; he had money to spend, women for the taking, and food that he could steal or that he could prepare for himself under a bridge.

For the several years, he lived his vagabond life on the run throughout the South. In the summer, he would roam through the North. At one time he signed on to work at a Carnival as it toured through the northern states. He soon discovered that working for the Carnival owners was nearly the same as being in the Army. He just did not like taking orders from anyone. When he became disillusioned with working for the circus, he returned to his life of raiding and pillaging. When the winter winds made it uncomfortable to sleep under a bridge or in someone's barn, he headed south where he was sure he could find a warm place to sleep.

LIFE IN GRIFFIN

Chapter forty-one

Hannah and her sons remained on the family farm that she was living on when Bartell had gone to the war. After Lydia was born, Hannah developed a helpmate in the house to assist in the household chores as the child grew. Taylor helped Mark and Luke clear more land to farm in order to raise more crops. Hannah raised hogs and butchered some for their own meat whenever the neighborhood farmers butchered theirs. Her sons would take the hogs to be butchered over to the butchering sight and stayed until their meat was ready. Most of the farmers who were butchering welcomed two extra hands to assist them in the messy job. Occasionally Mark was allowed to shoot the hogs to be butchered because he was such a crack-shot with a rifle.

Some of the neighbors knew that Hannah had young pigs to sell. She often sold off the ones that she did not need for food to other farmers in the community. This was extra money for her family's needs.

Her chickens were good 'layers' and the excess eggs that they produced brought her money when she sold them. Hannah had never expected to have money to spend but she did. As Mark and Luke worked the land, Taylor was able to help them learn more and more about how to have a productive farm.

The house that Hannah and her children were living in was beginning to become crowded. The boys were sleeping in the extra room that her father helped to build. Lydia and her mother were still sleeping on the straw tick in the corner. Hannah seemed to have a little extra money from the sale of her produce and meat. She asked Taylor if he could help her build another room on the other side of the building.

In the early spring of 1869, they began to work on building another room. Lydia was soon going to be seven years old, and she would share the new room with her mother. It was a big event to have more room for the family.

On one of her trips to Griffin, Hannah spied a big iron monstrosity that the man in the general store told her was a 'cook stove'. You could build a fire in it and cook on the top. Hannah had been cooking in the fireplace all these years, and she was not sure she could change her ways. She did not know about an oven or a reservoir on the side that would heat water as she was cooking. She talked to Taylor about this new-fangled invention, and he explained how it would work. He had seen them in his 'massa's' house. The clerk in the store told her that the stove would cost $35.00, and it would have to have a chimney flue. Taylor nodded his agreement for her to purchase the stove. He would be able to help her attach the stove to the fireplace chimney. Mark and Luke agreed to help move the heavy stove to the house. After a lot of tugging and lifting, the men managed to get the heavy stove into the wagon. Lydia and Hannah proudly rode in the wagon as they took the newest piece of equipment to be installed in their house. Hannah was confident that Taylor could also help her learn how to cook on it. As the men were unloading the stove in the kitchen, Hannah stood back, with pride, and announced that supper would be ready as soon as they could get a fire built in the big monstrosity that occupied most of the small room they used as a kitchen.

Chapter forty-two

Hannah soon mastered cooking on the cook stove in the kitchen. The new room was also finished, and the family was adjusting to all the new space that the room gave them.

Mark and Luke were growing up very fast. They were now in their early teens. They worked the fields in the summer, but tended to the cows, chickens and hogs all year. Mark hunted and fished during the winter to keep them in fresh meat. Taylor was still with them, and they considered him a part of the family although he slept in the barn at night unless it was bitter cold. If the temperature became very cold, Hannah could not bear the thought of him being in the barn. She would allow him to sleep in the kitchen by the cook stove. He would fire the stove during the night to help keep the family warm. She was never sure that he got much sleep when he was inside because he always seemed to be concerned about the family.

It was a bitter cold December day in 1869 when a rider came into the yard telling them that there was a barn fire over at another farm. Anyone who could help should go there.

Taylor, Mark, and Luke quickly got the wagon out and headed to the farm where the barn fire was. When they came near to the fire, they realized it was their grandfather's farm. The fire was raging in full force when they got there. The horses and the cows had been led from the flames to a nearby field.

All the men had formed a 'bucket brigade' from the local creek and made every attempt to try to douse the fire. However, it appeared that it would have to burn itself out. The neighbors continued to try to fight the fire for several hours, but the fire was more than the men could conquer. The men all discussed how the animals had been saved. Suddenly, it occurred to Mark that his grandfather was not anywhere around the house. He motioned for Luke to help him search for their grandfather. For more than two hours, the men of the area searched for the old man but he could not be found. The two boys sat on the steps of the house and discussed how they could tell their mother that her father probably had burned to death in the barn fire.

Taylor tied the cows to the wagon to lead them back to the house for Hannah. Mark and Luke mounted the two horses that had belonged to their grandfather and rode them home. The hogs and chickens would be gathered on the next day and taken to their home to add to their stock.

When Hannah was told the news of her father, she immediately broke down into torrents of tears. She had spent so little time with him since she had married. For the first few years of her married life, Bartell had refused to allow her to see her parents. After he left for the war, she was free to do as she pleased. It had been only a scant eight years of visiting with him and her mother. She realized that the time was not nearly long enough. She regretted that she had not spent more time with them. Now she would only be able to visit their grave in the cemetery.

When the morning light began to stream in her window, she realized that she would need to go to the church and ask for permission to bury her father near her mother. Suddenly she felt the emotion of being near the pastor again. Hannah did not want to have the warm feeling that she seemed to have when she was near him, but she was helpless to make it disappear. "I must think about my father," she said to herself. She quickly searched her closet for a clean dress. She wanted to look her best for the meeting with the pastor. She gathered up her long auburn hair in a bun at the back of her neck and pinched her cheeks to make them rosy. Maybe he would notice her, she thought. She was embarrassed at how much she was thinking of herself when she was supposed to be mourning the loss of her father.

Hannah hurried to the kitchen and prepared food for the family. While they were eating at the table, she announced her plan.

First, you must find any remains of my father in the ruins so that we can give him a decent burial.

"Then, Mark, you and Luke go back and hitch the horses to his wagon. You will need to take the wooden boxes to put the chickens in for bringing them over here, and whatever else you find," she said. "Taylor, you can help the boys, and you must get those hogs back here, somehow," she continued.

"I am going to the church to see if we can have a burial service tomorrow."

"Yes'm, ah can do that, but we ain got no body to be buryin'," Taylor added.

Hannah had not considered the fact that there was no body. Everyone assumed that her father had burned to death in the fire, but surely, there would be a body or parts of it, she thought.

"As I said earlier, your first job is to find the body, Taylor. I am sorry to give you such a gruesome task, but I can't expect the young boys to do it."

"Yes'm, ah seen lots of daid bodies."

The chores had been assigned and the men all left to do their jobs. Lydia would be left at home to cook the meals for the rest of us we returned. Hannah had asked that the mules be hitched to the wagon so that she could drive into Griffin to meet the pastor at the church. If they could not find at least part of her father's body, it would be appropriate to have just a memorial service and bury whatever parts they found in a grave next to her mother.

When Hannah arrived at the church, she entered the sanctuary and started to the part of the building where she knew the pastor would probably be. Before she could get there, he came out of his study and met her at the front of the church.

"I am so sorry to hear about your father, Mrs. Hauptman," he said as he approached her.

Hannah dropped her head to hide her tears. "Yes, I am sorry too; I will surely miss him. I am sorry that he had to die in a fire, but he would have wanted to save the animals. It appears that he sacrificed his life for the animals. Can I have him buried here in the cemetery near my mother's grave?" she asked.

"Of course," the pastor replied. "I felt sure that you would want to do so. I have already asked the men to begin to dig the grave. Because the ground is so frozen, it will be a full day before they can finish the grave. Is Tuesday a good day for the service?" the man asked.

Hannah hardly knew what day it was, so many things had happened lately. "Certainly, she replied, the boys and Taylor are over at the property gathering up the stock to move to my place. Tuesday will be fine."

The pastor walked over to Hannah and put his arm around her shoulders as he had done before. She began to feel warm inside again. "I shall be glad to have a service for you; do you think the 'black man' might sing again? I love hearing him sing in our Sunday service each week."

"Taylor has such a beautiful voice. I would be proud to have him sing for my father, if you think the townspeople will not disapprove."

"The community is very fond of you, Mrs. Hauptman, and they also know what a big help he has been to you, since your husband has not returned." "Have you heard anything from him? The war has been over for nearly five years. I know that it has been hard for you all these years, without your mate. God will honor you for your faithfulness to him." Hannah was surprised to hear the preacher ask about her husband. Surely, the townspeople knew that he had not returned after the war.

"No, I have not heard from him since he left in 1861. I guess it is reasonable to assume that his body is lying on some battlefield being consumed by the animals." Hannah shivered inside when she thought about that possibility, but she had no knowledge of what might have happened. It was strange to her to think that the Army had come and notified them of Sewell's death, and yet no one came to notify her of what might have happened to Bartell.

The pastor turned and faced her, looking into her face and said, "Someday, you will need to make a grave for him, too. I think it is reasonable to believe that he is not coming home again."

Hannah looked the preacher in the eye and saw a look of sympathy and of concern. She wondered if she saw compassion or possibly an interest in her as a woman. She noticed that she still had that same warm feeling inside when she looked into his face. She instantly dismissed the feeling until Bartell surfaced or the Army notified her she was still a married woman, legally. She admitted to herself that she had not really missed him since he had been so cruel to her when he was living in Griffin.

Chapter forty-three

Hannah buried her father's remains in the church cemetery next to her mother. The memorial service was short and accented by Taylor singing a hymn at the end after the preacher had delivered his message.

Mark and Luke had managed to gather up all the chickens except two or three. They just left them there thinking that someone would move into the house soon and would inherit two contrary old chickens.

Taylor had managed to get the old sow and her five pigs into her father's wagon and brought them home to her house. When he released the pigs into the pen with their hogs, it meant that he would soon have to enlarge the hog pen or butcher some of them. There were more hogs than the pen should hold. It was still cold enough to butcher, so Taylor related to Hannah that they might hold a butchering soon.

Hannah now had two wagons, three cows, two mules, three horses, several hogs and a big brood of chickens. She had more livestock than most people in the neighborhood.

The family returned to the Alstadt's place and brought some of the furniture home with them. Lydia's bed was taken to the barn for Taylor to use as his bed. Lydia received her grandmother's bed and dresser. Hannah took the chest of drawers that her parents had used for many years. The old round kitchen table that had been used in the Alstadt's kitchen was brought into Hannah's kitchen for her family to use. The board across two wooden boxes that Hannah has been using as a table was cut into firewood. When she realized how crowded their little house was getting, she wondered how she could have acquired so much so soon. She had a remarkable crew working for her on her little farm. Success seemed to be smiling on her.

Chapter forty-four

The spring of 1870 came in a hurry. It had been a bleak winter. The weather was unseasonably cold for longer than Hannah could remember. The root cellar was nearly depleted by the time spring came around. Taylor had helped them butcher two hogs in early January so they had a lot of meat, but the potatoes, turnips, carrots, beets, and the other root vegetables were all gone. Hannah still had some dried beans and a few cans of tomatoes that they could eat, but the variety was greatly diminished.

As soon as the tender shoots of greens showed themselves through the ground, Hannah and Lydia would go into the woods and forage for wild spring greens. Soon, they would plant radishes, lettuce, peas, and prepare their beds for other vegetable plants to set out as soon as the ground warmed a little bit.

Mark and Luke were going to be sixteen on their birthdays. They had faithfully attended school and had learned to read and write. They studied history, geography and arithmetic and shared what they had learned with the family. Some of the facts that the boys talked about were a complete mystery to Hannah. She was quite proud of her sons. They had grown into men through hard work on the farm. Taylor was their over-seer, and he was very much a part of the family. Hannah thanked God every day for such a fine man who happened onto her farm at a time when she needed him the most. She feared that he would leave any day. She never questioned him about leaving or staying; however, she wondered if he ever thought about his family that he had left behind when he ran away from the fierce hands of a slave owner. On the other hand, did he ever wish that he had a family of his own?

The family continued to attend church in Griffin. Mark and Luke had been baptized at the age of 13 following their conversions. They soon became leaders of the other young men and women in the church. Hannah remembered the times when she had attended the church at the age of 13. Those memories flooded her mind and then she remembered how they had turned into nightmares when she married Bartell.

Hannah was quite proud of her sons and daughter. But, she still had mixed emotions about her past. Sometimes she hoped the boys could remember the bad times and try not to be the same kind of person that their father had been. Other times she wanted them to forget the things that they had witnessed when they were quite small.

When Hannah began to reminisce about the times when Bartell lived with them, she realized again that he had been gone a long time. She had not thought about when or if he might return. She often wondered what his reaction would be when he saw what their sons and Taylor had accomplished while he was gone. And a shiver went up her spine when she thought about what he might do when he met his daughter, Lydia. She still had memories of what he had done to his first daughter, Sara. She was confident that her grown sons and Taylor would help her defend Lydia if Bartell ever chose to harm her.

Chapter forty-five

The Alstadt home place had stood empty for three years. A few people had inquired of Hannah if they could move into the house, but she always thought that she was not ready to let strangers live in her father's home.

Mark and Luke were nearly 20 years old and Hannah had noticed that Mark was attracted to a pretty girl at church by the name of Susan. Her family lived nearby. They had several other children. Susan seemed to be very ambitious and self-sufficient. Since she was the oldest, she had helped to raise her siblings while growing up in a busy household.

One evening, as the family finished their chores, Mark asked to speak to the family. Although Hannah was confident of what he would be saying, she was surprised when he gave her his news.

"I have been thinking, for a long time, about grandfather's farm, he began. It is standing empty and that is not good for a house or a farm. I would like to move into the house," he continued. While Hannah was thinking about his request, Mark went on with more news.

"I have never enjoyed farming like Luke does, he said. I am a hunter and a trapper by choice. I have been offered the opportunity to work at Stamper's Mill in town," Mark continued. "He will pay me a wage and allow me to hunt and trap during the winter months. I can sell the furs at the mill for extra money. I know the farm does not have a barn, but I do not plan to have farm animals. Luke can continue to farm the land for you, Mother. All that I want is a place to live," Mark stated, rather succinctly.

"It would appear that you have thought this through, Mark. I guess that I do not have any objection to my son living in the house," Hannah stated. "Am I to assume that you may take a wife soon? I know that you have been paying extra attention to Susan Stamper."

"Well, Mother, Mark continued, you are very astute. Yes, when her father offered me a job, and I did not have to concentrate on being a farmer the rest of my life, I considered the fact that I would ask her to marry me. She is a fine young woman and will make me a wonderful wife," and with that statement he walked over to Luke and smiled. "You can be the Hauptman farmer, little brother."

Luke had remained silent while Mark was

stating his case about the farmhouse. He already knew about the job offer at the Mill because Mark had discussed it with him. Now that the plan was out in the open, Luke spoke up and agreed to help Mark get settled in the empty farmhouse.

Lydia also spoke up and said that she would cook an extra meal for Mark once in awhile to keep him from starving. She giggled a bit when they talked about a wedding with Susan. However, Lydia stood and announced that she would help make the wedding dress if Susan wanted her help.

"It looks as if my children have made all the plans and do not need my help in this adventure," Hannah said. "I guess the only thing that I need to ask is when will it all take place?"

"I would like to move into the house soon," Mark said.

"You already have my permission, son. Luke and Taylor will start working on the property tomorrow." Hannah turned and walked into her bedroom to hide her tears of joy when she realized that her sons were now adults.

Chapter forty-six

The summer of 1872 was winding down. The Fall weather was rapidly approaching. Most of the fall crops had been harvested and put in the root cellar or else they had been stored in the barn. Hannah was sure that they had enough food to feed them all winter if the weather did not turn too severe.

One evening, as Hannah and Lydia were sitting by the fireplace, there seemed to be a big commotion outside. They could hear the chickens squawking and the horses seemed to be restless. The old hound dog heralded the news that someone was nearby. Luke came from his room with his shotgun in his hands and started out the door to protect the family. Before he could get the door opened, Taylor knocked his familiar knock on the door. Luke opened the door to see what was wrong.

"Miz Hannah, can ah sees you a minute? He asked.

"Of course, Taylor, what is wrong," she asked.

"Miz Hannah, dere is a fambly of darkies goin' north, and dey wanna stay in de barn, tonight.

Is dat awright wit you?"

"Taylor, you may bring them in; are they hungry? Lydia, warm up the stew."

"Miz Hannah, dey is five ub dem. A mamma, a dad, a girl, and 2 chilluns."

"It does not matter, Taylor; I want them to have a good meal. We will get blankets and bedding for them to sleep tonight, but first, I want them to eat with us," Hannah insisted. "Now don't argue with me, just go get them and bring them in to get warm by the fire."

Taylor fairly flew out the door and back to the barn to get the family. They all crowded into the kitchen and gathered around the table for stew, biscuits and a chocolate cake that Lydia had baked during the day. Even though the biscuits were left from breakfast they family did not seem to care.

Hannah made a pot of coffee for all the adults, and gave the children large glasses of milk to drink. It was clear that this family had not eaten a meal in several days.

When the meal was finished, Hannah sat down at the table and talked with the strangers.

"I am not being nosey, she began, but I am just curious about where you are going? It will be winter up north very soon," she continued.

The black man bowed his head and spoke first. "Ah'm tryin' ta fin a home for my daughter and her chillins'," he said. "She ain got no man. He dun left her two years back, I knowed if I cud git up north, we'd fin a job."

The girl hung her head but gathered her little children around her. She looked so desperate that her demeanor tore at Hannah's heartstrings. This child could well have been herself if Taylor had not happened to come by her farm, so many years ago. No doubt, he had been heaven sent!

Hannah walked to the girl's side and put her arm around the black girl. She could see the warmth in the eyes of this woman who was very little more than a child herself. The expression on the face of the black woman was one of gratitude for someone who seemed to understand her plight.

"Taylor will make arrangements for you in the barn. I am sorry that I do not have room for you in the house, but I will make sure you are warm and dry for the night. Tomorrow we will have a big breakfast for you and discuss what your plans might be for your future," Hannah said, as she reached out to touch the mother's arm. Don't worry about tonight, we will help you tomorrow."

The black man and woman helped the girl

take her children out the back door to the barn. Lydia and Luke followed them with blankets and quilts to help them have a bed. Hannah smiled when she saw Luke hand over his bearskin to the little boy so that he could sleep under it for at least one night.

As soon as everyone had settled as well as they could, Hannah heard a slight knock on the door again. She slowly opened the door to see that Taylor was back to see her. "Is there something wrong, Taylor?" she asked.

"Oh, no, ma'am, dere's no problem. Ah came to say thank you; You's been so kind to dese strangers. I was jus wonderin, do you think I could ask the girl and dem chillun to stay? Dey needs a home. She's mighty purty an strong too. She'd be good help fo you an miz Lydia. Ah ain got nobody but me, an I cud make her a good home. If'n you let me, ah cud build us a lean to on the barn to live in."

"Oh, Taylor, you are a soft hearted old man. Of course, you can let her and her children stay. We will work on all those problems in the daylight. Now go on to the barn and get some sleep," Hannah replied with firmness.

As Taylor walked out the door, Hannah realized that this man had been all alone for most of his life. He had never experienced the warmth of a woman lying near him in bed. He had not had the opportunity to whisper in her ear how he felt about her. She remembered how he had helped her birth Lydia, but she was convinced that he had not seen the anatomy of a woman of his own. In addition, he had never fathered a child of his own so he did not know the pride a man would have in his own offspring.

As she stood in the doorway that Taylor had just walked out of, she realized that she had not had those same experiences of her own. She had never had the warmth of a man in bed with her except when she had been beaten to submission. No man had ever whispered in her ear any terms of endearment. However, her pride and joy were the children that Bartell had given her even though they were conceived through lust. The only other gift that he had ever given her was a pair of scissors that his daughter now used every day to pursue her love of sewing.

Hannah turned and walked into her bedroom and lay down on her bed while she longed for the love of a man to hold her and comfort her in her loneliness. She turned her head toward the wall and slowly fell asleep while the tears were still wet on her pillow.

Chapter forty-seven

When morning came, a soft knock came at the door, again. Hannah opened the door to see the lovely young mother standing on the stoop. "Ah came to help, she said. Taylor said I should be in the kitchen cooking with you and your girl."

"Well, no one can help in this kitchen without me knowing your name, ma'am."

"My name is Cleo, the girl said. Cleo Patterson. My husband left me a long time ago, but I kept his name. We waren't rightly married cause we dint know any preacher. We just said a few words to each other, and played like we wuz married."

"Do you know where he went?" Hannah asked. "No, ma'm, he dun left one night; said he was goin' north, and be back to git me, but he never come',"

"Well, we will just assume that he isn't coming back. If you will take that stack of plates over there and set the table, we will get these biscuits and gravy on the table, soon. Those men are going to be starving when they hit this kitchen. Is your mother well?" Hannah asked.

"Yes'm, she be fine. Her an my dad have fambly up north, dey say. I dunno, I never hab seen any, but dey say so."

The men came in just as Lydia and Cleo had everything ready on the table. Lydia had prepared a gallon crock of gravy, baked three pans of biscuits, fried a large platter of ham, and had dried apples for everyone.

Cleo gathered her children together and filled their plates. It appeared that the children were not twins but they were very close in age. Cleo called the children by their names, Willa Mae and Hershel, as she seated them on the backside of the table. Taylor hovered over Cleo as if he were a mother hen. He smiled at her each time he looked in her direction. Hannah was amused at his demeanor around this woman who had happened into his life quite by accident less than 24 hours ago.

As soon as breakfast was over, the men went back to the barn. The father remained in the kitchen for a few moments and asked to speak to Hannah. She dried her hands on her crisp apron and turned in his direction.

"Ah wan to thank you fo yo kindness, he said. My fambly is ever so grateful fo yo food and bed. Cleo is wantin to stay with Taylor, he continued, is dat ok wit you?"

"Taylor has been a real blessing to me and my family, Hannah began. He came here shortly after my husband went off to the war. I would have been alone with no one to help me, but Taylor came in the middle of the night, just as you did, and I considered him a gift from God. He is a hardworking, clean living, generous and gentle man. He came to me last night and asked my permission to allow Cleo to stay with him. I am sure that he would never harm your daughter and would provide for those children as if they were his own. He will give them everything that he is capable of earning for them. I assured him that I would help him in his effort to build a place for them to live on the property. I can not pay him a lot of money, nor can I pay your daughter for any help that she gives me in the house, but I will allow them a place to live, food to grow for themselves, and help them school those children at the nearby school if the community allows it."

The old black man shook her hand as the tears rolled down his face. "Ah'l never forget you, he said. God bless you and all your fambly," he mumbled, as he walked out of the door to the waiting wagon loaded with his family's belongings. He took the reins in his leathered hands as they headed north into the bright sunrise. Cleo and Taylor waved goodbye knowing that they would never to see them again. Willa Mae and Hershel were busy playing with the dog and chasing the chickens completely oblivious to what the future would hold for them.

Chapter forty-eight

Taylor, Luke, and Cleo walked over the farm area looking for a place where they could build them a home. Just at the edge of the woods there seemed to be a little flat part of the land.

"Let's put a rock here, Taylor said, and call this our home place. Is dat ok wit you, Cleo?" Taylor asked.

"Any place you say, Taylor. I'm just glad to find a place to stay," Cleo replied.

"You know I ain got much," Taylor tried to tell her, but she just ignored his denial. "Miz Hannah dun give me all I have," he stated.

"I don wanna hear no more, Cleo said. Wha we got is wha we got. Now, les go ask Miz Hannah for her permission to start on our house." It was a good thing that most of the fall chores had been done because the work started on the Taylor/Cleo house almost immediately.

Luke had gone to the Mill to tell Mark about the events of the last two days. Mr. Stamper heard the conversation and mentioned that he had a pile of old lumber behind the building if they wanted to use it. Luke and Taylor gratefully loaded it on the wagon and took it back home with them. They went into the field to find large stones to use as the corner stones for the house. The house would only be a lean-to with enclosed sides, for the first winter. They would need to put a roof on the structure to keep out the weather. As material became available, they would add more space to the building in the spring. At least for the present time, they would have a roof over their head.

While the men were busy in the construction project, Cleo and Lydia worked with the children trying to get them acquainted with their new family.

Hannah wanted to take the children to church with her on Sunday, but she wanted the pastor to know, in advance, that there would be a black family, in addition to Taylor, that would be coming to the church. Moreover, she wanted the opportunity to see the pastor again.

Hannah went into her room and found a clean dress. She tied up her auburn hair and powdered her nose a bit. She wanted to look her best. She splashed on a bit of 'toilet water' that she had purchased at the store a few weeks ago. She wanted the pastor to notice her when she arrived at the church. Hannah was very excited at the prospects of seeing the pastor again. Each time she thought about him, she got the same 'warm feeling'. She could not identify it, but she knew it was real.

When she reached the church, she walked over to the cemetery to visit the graves of her parents. She began to talk to them as if they were standing by her side. "Mother, the boys are grown and Lydia is a beautiful girl, she began. Mark has a job in town, and Luke is still farming both farms. Mark has moved into your house. He does not want to be a farmer. He will be getting married soon, and Lydia is going to help Susan Stamper make her wedding gown. We have a family of 'darkies' living on the back of our farm. They will help me on the farm. I wish that you could see how well we have done on that old piece of ground. Bartell has never come home. I do not know where he is, or if he will ever be back. I hope that I can start over now," Hannah continued.

"I certainly hope so," a voice from behind her said. Hannah did not hear the pastor come walking up. "You have waited far too long for him to return," the pastor said.

Hannah blushed when she realized that the pastor had heard her confess that she was ready to start over without her husband.

The pastor put his arm around her shoulders

as he always did and asked her to come inside the church. They could talk quietly inside, he said.

Hannah gladly went inside with the pastor. He opened the door for her and brushed against her as she walked inside with him.

She explained the story about Cleo and the two children that Taylor had agreed to take. She wanted to bring them to church, but she did not want the community to do anything that would embarrass the new citizens of Griffin.

The pastor assured her that he would handle any complaints that the people might have. He was convinced that they would open their hearts to homeless children regardless of the color.

Hannah stood to leave the church, and as she did, the pastor reached for her hand. He held it in his for a few seconds then he stooped and kissed her forehead as she was leaving. She smiled and assured him that she would return soon.

She stepped up in the wagon and headed down the road to the farm. When she crossed over the old bridge, she again looked into the swirling waters and smiled. She was sure that her life was about to turn around.

Chapter forty-nine

Bartell had been a renegade, riding and pillaging homes from the war zone into the Kansas territory. He had managed to survive with food that he had stolen from farms and farmhouses. He could catch a chicken, find a bridge over a stream, build a fire and have chicken for supper; or he could find a house with a Negro cook, enter the summer kitchen, and hold the cook at knifepoint until she gave him all the food that he would need for a few days. He had been sleeping in barns, taking a fresh horse when he left, leaving his worn out old nag for the farmer in exchange for another steed. In addition, on occasion, he would find a southern plantation with a wife at home where he could assault her in her clean white bed, rob her of her jewels, and leave before the husband returned home or the black manservant realized what was happening.

When he happened into a town called St. Louis, he found out more about trains. He could board a train in the cattle car, ride to the next town, do his dastardly deeds and hop another freight train going the other way before sundown.

Bartell never before realized that this lifestyle could be so easy for a natural born thief. He was happy with the life he was cutting out for himself. He never gave much thought to the life that he left behind in Griffin. That community and the life he had there only seemed to represent hard work and drudgery. He never wanted to work as hard as that life had demanded in Posey County, Indiana.

Most of the time that Bartell served in the war he spent either as a cook or as a scout behind enemy lines. He was not a very good cook, but he was an excellent scout. If a Rebel soldier got in his way, he simply used his Bowie knife on him and went on to see if he could discover what the enemy was planning next.

When the war ended, Bartell headed back to Indiana. Then he had realized that he would be returning to a life of hard work and bad luck, if the weather did not cooperate. One of the men that he had fought with in the Army mentioned to him that he was considering becoming a wanderer; he asked Bartell if he would like to join him in his travels across the Midwest. His friend, Eldon, explained what they could do to earn money to support them, and Bartell quickly realized that it seemed to be an easier life than working on the farm.

Eldon and Bartell traveled together for the first few years after the war, but soon Eldon finally became disillusioned with their lifestyle, and he decided to go home to northern Indiana. Bartell continued on, alone.

He often encountered people on the trains that were also on the run. Some of them were vagabonds from the War. Bartell was never sure which side they had been fighting for so he just kept silent about his own background. If they were Rebels, they might make an effort to kill him. If they were Union soldiers, they were in the same business that Bartell was pursuing and they might be his competition for his next meal. He found it best not to ask any questions of any of the people that he encountered.

Bartell continued his chosen lifestyle for the next few years. He wandered across many miles and saw many towns where the residents were living just as he had lived in Griffin. They, too, were poor and barely eking out a living on a piece of barren ground. The shopkeepers were selling their wares to the poor residents in hopes that someday the crops would come in and they would be paid in real money for a measly pound of coffee or beans. When the crops did not come in, the merchants were often paid with chickens or eggs. Bartell did not want to return to that kind of a life. He preferred to rob and steal for his survival.

One day, shortly before noon, he wandered into a saloon in a small town outside of St. Louis. He had just jumped off a train as it was pulling into the station. He had a knapsack full of jewelry and cash which he always carried with him. He also had a small pistol and a Bowie knife hidden in his belt. He found a small table over in the corner of the saloon and asked the bar maid for some grub. As she left to go to the kitchen to get his food, he began to listen to the other men talking. They seemed agitated about something that was about to take place in the town square.

When the bar maid returned with his plate of beans and meat, and he was running his hand up her backsides he asked what the commotion was all about in town. She moved his hand off her butt and smiled at him, saying: "They are going to hang a man at noon today."

"For what," quizzed Bartell.

"He is a horse thief," she replied. "We don't 'cotton' to them around here."

Bartell hurriedly ate his meal, left her a tip, and quickly forgot about his earlier thoughts that he would come back for a quick roll in the hay with her.

He left the saloon and started down the street in the opposite direction of the hanging. He hurried back to the train station to see when the next locomotive might be passing through town. He decided that this town was not one that he wanted to stay in very long.

Bartell slipped around to the back of the train station and waited for everyone on the sidewalk to get out of sight before he ventured around to the front of the building. He wanted to see the board that listed the arrivals and departures. He wanted to head east so he looked to see if he could get out of this 'hangin' town before sundown.

He saw that the listing on the board said the next train to St. Louis would be there in about an hour. Bartell sat down on the bench outside the station with his hat pulled low over his unruly red hair and thought that he would wait until the train came. He hoped that no one would notice him. He feared that his past was beginning to catch up with him. However, it was not long before people began to arrive to read the same board that had interested Bartell. He did not want to be noticed by this crowd. He had to make a move.

It was a very hot afternoon in the middle of July, 1870. The street that ran by the railroad station was dirt, and dusty from the hooves of a hundred horses that had run through town in the last few days. Bartell wanted the train to hurry and carry him away from the town where they hanged horse thieves. He wanted no one to suspect that he was a horse thief, although he had left his worn out steed that he had stolen several miles back, outside the saloon where he had eaten his first good meal in several days. He knew the man that owned that horse was several miles back and that he would never discover it. He was sure that he looked like any other drifter that came to town on a hot dusty day.

Bartell was afraid to sit on the bench in front of the station. He cautiously sneaked around to the side of the station and hid in the shadows away from the early afternoon sun. From his vantage point, if he saw someone coming, he could drift further into the shadows of the building. He thought about how bad he needed a bath. If he ever got out of this town, he would look for a river or stream where he could take a cold bath and forget his worries.

It was nearly 2:00 P.M. when Bartell heard the train whistle in the distance. He was not sure that it would stop in such a small town, but it was sure to slow down. He hurried around the building to the backside of the station and began to hurry down the track, going in the same direction as the train. He wanted to have his momentum going when he tried to hop on the moving train. He was quite adept at jumping into a cattle car or any open door on the train if it only slowed. He knew what he needed to do. Experience had taught him how to prepare for the jump.

When the eastbound train came into town, as Bartell had expected, it slowed for the street crossings. He was not sure where the train had come from or where it was going, but he knew that he wanted to be on it. His past was about to catch up with him. If the crowd, who was hanging the horse thief, found out that he was one also, he knew what his fate would be.

He casually got up from the bench and started a slow run to gather the same speed as the train. He planned to leap up, grab the side of the door, and swing his body and his knapsack into the train car. However, something went awry. Bartell lost his footing and he began to stumble. He could not swing his body up into the train car as the train began to pick up speed. He lost his grip on the door and he fell to the ground. His right leg fell onto the track and the train cars ran over it, as the locomotive sped out of sight.

Bartell rolled over in the dirt and began to yell in pain. The stationmaster had witnessed the accident and came to aid the injured man. A by-stander hurried to get a doctor to see what could be done for the stranger. Judging from the amount of blood that was in the dirt, this stranger was in danger of bleeding to death if he did not get help soon. A stranger took the belt off Bartell and made a 'make-shift' tourniquet to slow the flow of blood from the stump of his leg.

When the doctor arrived, he told the gathering crowd to take the man to his office. He would assess the injury and see what could be done for the patient.

Bartell began to shout that he did not want to lose his leg. He wanted to be left whole. Most of the people standing around knew that his foot and part of his leg were still on the railroad bed. Only the screaming man knew that he did not have a leg.

At the doctor's office, the doctor administered some ether to the patient to calm him. Dr. Euler removed the ragged pants from the stub and began to look for a method to stop the bleeding. A farmer from the saloon stepped up to the doctor's table and offered to assist him. They heated the cauterizing iron over an open flame and used it to stop the bleeding. The farmer tried to wash away some of the Missouri dirt from the open wound. The patient was blissfully asleep as they prepared to cauterize the stump that once had a leg and foot attached to it.

When the Bartell awoke, he soon realized that his leg was gone, just below the knee. He was angry and began to swear at the doctor and the man who had helped him. He was in excruciating pain. He could smell the odor in the room and he knew that it was the smell of his burning flesh. Bartell knew that the doctor had used the heated iron to sear the ends of his blood vessels and nerves to stop the bleeding. He lay back down on the table and slowly began to think about his past life. Now, it was apparent that he would never be able to continue doing the things that he had been doing. His life as a renegade was over.

Doctor Euler asked the lady at the boarding house if she could make room for Bartell. It would be several weeks before he would be able to walk again. Bartell's stump would have to heal completely before he could be fitted with a peg leg. During the time that his leg was healing, he would be unable to do much, but could he stay with her?

Mrs. Bould agreed to make him a place in her

rooming house and give him something to eat each day. "Does he have any money?" she asked.

"He has a knapsack full of jewelry and cash," the farmer quickly answered. "There is enough there to keep him for a long time."

Mrs. Bould smiled and decided that he might be her best paying customer for the next few months. She would assess how long it would take him to get well just as soon as she could find out how much money was in the knapsack.

Bartell was moved to the boarding house by the farmer and the doctor. Dr. Euler agreed to check on his patient every day for a few weeks. He asked Mrs. Bould if she could assist him in dressing the wound. Her response was that she would do the best she could; however, treating dirty old men was not her specialty. "When can I give him a bath?" she asked.

"I'll come by tomorrow," replied the farmer, "and help clean him up a bit."

Bartell spent the next few months in the home of Mrs. Bould. Even though she was a rather attractive woman, he was not interested in her charms. He was very distraught about his fate. He wanted to blame everyone except himself for his predicament. When the stationmaster came by to pay his respects to Bartell, the man simply shook his head in dismay when Bartell tried to blame the accident on the man who had watched him try to get on the train without a ticket.

Bartell had completely forgotten about the hanging of the horse thief that had taken place in the town the afternoon of his accident.

It was eight months before Bartell could manage to get around. One afternoon, as Bartell was sunning himself on the front porch of the boarding house, Mrs. Bould brought him a glass of lemonade. She sat down in the rocking chair beside him and began to try to talk to him. He had refused to talk to anyone prior to this afternoon.

"That is a beautiful pocket watch that you have," she stated.

"What pocket watch are you talking about," Bartell growled.

"The one that you had in your knapsack along with your confederate money. It has a lovely ladies picture in the front of the case," she continued. "Is she your wife?"

Bartell turned his head away. He had not thought about his wife in many years. He was not sure that he still had one. Maybe she had died. Maybe she had married someone else.

"Yes, she is my wife," he lied and said. "She was burned to death in a fire," he continued.

Mrs. Bould suspected that Bartell was lying to her. If she had been his wife, the watch would have been in his own pocket, not stuck in the bag with his other stuff. Now she knew the truth. This man was a thief. She vowed that she would hide her family's silver somewhere so that he could not find it. In addition, she decided to carry her cash in her under-drawers until he left. Bartell stayed with Mrs. Bould for nearly two more years. But, from that time forward, she never trusted him out of her sight.

As Bartell's leg slowly began to heal, he had to learn how to walk on the peg leg that the doctor had given him. He began to walk on it a little each day. It was quite painful, since Bartell had resisted using it; however, he did not like being unable to get around. Eventually, he 'set his jaw' in determination that he would master the miserable appendage. Soon he was able to walk with it for quite a distance.

Bartell's money was gone. It took all the money that he had with him to pay the doctor and Mrs. Bould. He needed to find work. But what could a man with one leg do to earn money? Mrs. Bould had passed the word around town that she did not think that he had told her the truth about his wife. Since the shopkeepers believed her story, they were reluctant to give their stranger access to any money. The man at the livery stable offered him the opportunity to work there cleaning the stalls and tending the animals. Bartell hated the thought of doing common labor, but his money was gone and Mrs. Bould wanted to be paid for room and board. He took the job and found that he was able to walk on his peg leg rather well. He and the horses became good friends. Bartell also noted when someone who had a stolen horse came into the livery stable. He could usually tell by the rider's demeanor. He was convinced that they were 'shifty-eyed' and constantly looking over their shoulders. He also noted that they were careful not to look anyone in the eye as they spoke. He was sure these were the marks of a horse-thief, perhaps because these traits had been his own in the past. He chose not to mention to anyone, his suspicions. He was convinced that his past would catch up with him if he revealed what he felt about another stranger. Bartell did his job in silence.

Chapter fifty

Bartell really wanted to get out of this little town. He realized that perhaps it was time for him to go home. He convinced himself that if he went back to Griffin, Hannah would take care of him. She was strong and healthy. She would care for him and give him some sympathy. She and their sons probably had that farm running in tip-top shape. The boys were nearly 20 years old now and were old enough to be farmers in their own right.

Although he had decided to go back to Griffin, he did not have any idea as to how he could get there. He certainly did not want to risk trying to hop a freight train again, since the last time he tried that he lost a leg. And, now, he could not run at a steady pace. He did not have any money and had no idea of how he could get money. It took every penny that he earned at the livery stable to pay Mrs. Bould and to eat his meals at the local saloon.

Bartell began to think about how he could find a way to get out of town. He knew that he would not be able to steal from anyone in town since everyone knew him as the man with a peg leg. However, he did have one idea. He had seen that when Mrs. Bould had women in for teas on certain afternoons each month, she set her tables with silver. When she prepared a tea, her table was set with fine china and crystal. That is when he also noticed that she had a vast array of silver service. He saw the silver tea service and a large silver punch bowl. However, he noticed that the silver was never put away in the china cabinet. He could not help but wonder where she stored the silver. If he could find her hiding place, maybe he could take it and head out of town before she realized that he had taken it. If he could possibly get to St. Louis, he was convinced that he could sell it for enough money to get home to Griffin.

Bartell watched the landlady carefully but he could not seem to find where she might be hiding the silver. He certainly hoped that she was not storing it under her bed, since he would never have the opportunity to look for it there. When he was home, she stayed in her room, unless she sat with him on the porch in the swing. She seemed to have her eye on him at every waking moment that he was in her house.

Bartell was a patient man. He waited for her to reveal where she might be storing her valuables including the silver.

Each evening after working all day at the livery stable, Bartell would stop by the saloon for his evening meal. Then he would hobble home to the boarding house. One evening as he was coming up the back stairs, he noticed that the root cellar door was open. He went back down the steps and started to close the door to the root cellar. If the door was not closed, animals could get inside and eat the food that Mrs. Bould had carefully stored for the winter. As Bartell was closing the door, he noticed a large black box over in the corner of the cellar. He was sure that he had never seen this box before. He had been with Mrs. Bould for almost three years, and he knew her habits rather well. He carefully hobbled over to the black box and lifted the lid. Inside the box were several large packages wrapped in quilts and blankets. Bartell carefully unwrapped one of the packages and discovered what he had been looking for; he found the elusive silver and the method for him to leave town.

He wrapped the package again and slowly closed the door to the root cellar. He continued up the back stairs and into the house. He slowly went to his room and closed the door. He began to gather his clothes together and made plans for what he would take with him on his escape. He did not have many personal belongings. Therefore, his plans to go back to Griffin took only a few short minutes to put together.

He lay across his bed and began to make mental plans for his journey. He knew that he could get a good horse for his trip from the livery stable. He did not want to steal it because it would arouse too much suspicion. He was not as agile or as swift as he was in the past, and he was afraid that he could not escape as quickly as he would like. He would have to decide just how to get out of town legally but with the silver. He had a payday coming up on Saturday. If he used his wages, perhaps he could buy a horse; but he might not have enough to buy a very good horse. However, if he bought the horse, he would not need a very good one to get to St. Louis where he could sell the silver. In addition, he would need to make his escape after Mrs. Bould had her next tea for her lady-friends. Then he would probably have two or three weeks before she would need to use the silver again. By that time, he would be almost all the way back to Griffin. After he sold the silver, he could get a train to take him to Southwest Indiana or even a better horse to ride the rest of the way home. He seemed to have the foolproof plan all formulated in his head. He would make sure that he had his own belongings in order. He decided that the best thing to do was to put all of his clothes on, one layer on top of another layer. Everything else that he owned could be stashed in his pockets. He knew that he could choose a horse, use his wages to pay for it, but leave it at the livery stable until he could get the bundles of silver. He planned to go to the root cellar for the silver as soon as it was dark that night. He would then go back to the stable and ride off into the dark toward Griffin, Indiana. Bartell was off to a new chapter in his life.

Chapter fifty-one

Hannah was always very busy at the farm. She was helping Taylor and Cleo work on their little house up on the hill. There was not a surplus of furniture in her home, but she was willing to share with the young family what she had. Since Mark had gone, his bed was still empty in the room where Luke was sleeping. She agreed to give it to the new family. She gathered a few blankets and quilts that she had brought from her parents home when they cleaned out the house after the family was buried. She gave them to the black family so they would have something to use when the winter winds came. Luke and Taylor put a fireplace in the little shanty to provide warmth in the winter, and to provide a place where Cleo could cook meals for the family.

Winter was just around the corner and the temperature would soon be dropping. Most of the fall chores were completed, and all the efforts of the family were concentrated on getting the shanty completed before bad weather arrived. Lydia had helped by making clothes for the little ones. She found a coat that had belonged to her grandmother and made a coat and hat for Willie May. Cleo did not have a heavy coat, so Lydia was given the challenge of making a warm coat for her out of the old coats of her own family. When the family had left their home in the south, they did not have winter coats. Therefore, Lydia continued to rummage through the clothes that had belonged to her grandparents looking for fabric that she could make into something for the black family to wear during the winter months. Hershel also needed a coat; Lydia found her grandfather's coat and cut it down to fit him.

Willie May and Hershel were attending school at the same place where Lydia was going. They all went together in a wagon. She was like a mother hen to those little 'darkie' children. She hovered over them and protected them from the other schoolchildren who would taunt them about being in a school of all white children. Lydia protected them by saying that they wanted to learn to read and write just like all other children. She also mentioned to the others that the preacher at their church allowed the 'darkies' to attend the church services. "Why shouldn't they be allowed to go to school?" she questioned. The teacher was a young woman who lived in Griffin. She knew the Haup
tman family, and that Hannah had made a life for her

family without a man in the house. When the teacher saw this young woman defend the little black children, she immediately agreed with her and allowed the little 'darkies' to attend her school to learn to read and write. Lydia became the defender of her little charges and she was almost a surrogate mother to them when they were away from home. Even though Lydia was only 12 years old, her motherly instinct was quite remarkable.

Chapter fifty-two

While Hannah and the rest of the family worked on the shanty for the black family, Lydia was busily working on the wedding dress for Mark's bride, Susan. Susan had ordered the satin from a mail order house in St. Louis that Lydia would use for her dress. The dress would have lace up and down the front and around the bottom. The bustle in the back would also be covered in lace. It would take many yards of lace for all these areas. Lydia was working feverishly on making all the lace that she would need to trim the dress.

Winter was just around the corner and Lydia would need to have the dress finished by spring before the planting season began. She was expecting to work on the dress during the cold winter months because she did not have many other chores to do.

It had been raining for several days. The creeks were flooded and the fields were wet. The men had put a roof on the shanty just in time to beat the winter rains. Taylor, Cleo and the children would have a warm and dry place to live this winter.

It seemed that everyone in the extended family

of Hannah and her children had settled in awaiting winter.

Chapter fifty-three

The weather was turning bad on Bartell as he was trying to make his way back to Griffin. He had managed to sell the silver in St. Louis, but had to take less than he thought it was worth. He did not have much choice in the matter since he was penniless. He needed cash to buy a fresh horse and he had not eaten in several days. The old nag that he had purchased at the livery stable was barely able to make it through the day. Bartell did not want to spend his money for a night's rest, so he was sleeping under bridges, just as he had done for many years. He could get a good meal for twenty-five cents at most saloons whether it was breakfast or supper. Therefore, he felt he could eat well and sleep wherever he could find a spot without spending much of his cash. It had been a long time since he had concentrated his thinking about what his future would bring; now he was seriously wondering about what life would be like for him in Griffin.

He came to the river bank of the Kaskaskia River in rural Illinois and knew that he was getting near to the life that he left so long ago. He saw that the rains had caused the river to rise. He contemplated whether the horse could make it across the swollen and fast moving water. If the horse could not make it across, he would need to go north to the ferry at St. Francisville. Suddenly he realized that he was anxious to get back to the life he left behind nearly thirteen years ago.

The river was too swift for Bartell to trust it. He hated fast moving waters. The strength and power of a river stream frightened him. He had a fear of drowning. He never had admitted to being afraid of anything, but looking down into the moving water brought back old feelings of fear. He decided that he would ride the horse on up to the ferry and go across the river safely. It would cause him to lose a day of travel time, but he was convinced that the delay was worth it to arrive safely.

As soon as he crossed into Indiana from the ferry ride, he knew that it would not be long before he found his way home.

Chapter fifty-four

Hannah was down at the barn collecting the eggs from the old laying hens when she noticed a strange horse tied up at the tree in front of the house. She wondered who could be stopping by her place. She started to go into the other part of the barn when she thought that she heard Lydia screaming. She stopped for a second to listen and sure enough, she could hear her shouting at someone. She put the egg basket on a tree stump and hurried to the house. As she neared the house, she could hear Lydia's crying for help. Hannah rushed into the house, ran to Luke's room and got the rifle. She hurried into Lydia's room to find a grizzly looking man on top of her trying to rip her clothes off.

Hannah raised the rifle and cocked the hammer back. It was at that instant, she realized the grizzly looking man was Bartell. "Stop, you fool; don't you realize that she is your daughter. Stop or I will shoot you right now. You will not shame our child by your own selfish lusts, like you did me."

Bartell stopped in his efforts to rape Lydia and started to stand up. He had forgotten that he had taken his peg leg off when he took off his breeches. He tried to step down but he stumbled as he put his stump on floor. It caused him to be unbalanced. He fell across the sewing basket where Lydia had been working on Susan's dress. Hannah's silver scissors pierced his throat at the jugular vein. His half-naked body fell onto the floor and his blood was spurting across the floor with each heartbeat, the scissors still extending from his throat. Hannah laid the gun aside and went to her husband's body. She looked into his eyes and watched him clutch at his neck. He was trying to talk to her but the blood was gurgling in his throat; his voice was coming out in garbled sounds. He was trying to pull the scissors from his throat, but he did not have the strength to complete the act.

"Go get Taylor, and you stay with Cleo and the children," Hannah yelled to her daughter. "I'll handle this," she continued. "Just tell Taylor that I need him now." NOW!

"Where have you been for the last thirteen years? Why did you decide to come back to us?" While she was screaming questions at Bartell, his blood was spurting from his body onto the carpet in her bedroom. Hannah did not know what else to do. She did not think she could save his life; the flow of his blood was slowing and his grizzly face was beginning to look pale.

Taylor stepped into the room and saw the man, whom he had never met, lying in the floor. He was shocked to see the nakedness of the man, but surmised what had happened. He saw that Hannah was distraught. She had begun to cry. He knelt beside her and tried to calm her crying. "I think it is too late fo him, ma'am. Wha ya want me ta do, miz Hannah? Dis man is daid!"

Hannah rose to her feet and wiped her bloody hands on her apron. She glanced down at the father of her children whom she had not seen in a very long time. Somehow, she felt no pity. She surprised herself when she glanced at his filthy, naked body, and felt only disgust.

"Let's roll him up in the carpet," she said. "You go get the wagon, and I will put his clothes on him. I cannot stand to see him naked like this. He also needs a bath," Hannah continued.

Hannah picked up the knapsack that Bartell had thrown in the corner. She decided that she would check to see what was in the bag. She found only small golden snuffbox with an initial "C" on the top, and a few Confederate dollars.

When Taylor brought the wagon around to the door, she helped him load the body into the wagon.

"Let's go down to the bridge," Hannah said.

As the two of them traveled in silence, Hannah was thinking back over the many years that he had been gone. She and the men in her life had developed a nice size farm. It was supporting them quite well. She was educating her children without Bartell's help. She had helped a runaway slave develop a life, given a new start in life to a young black family, and now she could have a life of her own.

As Taylor drove the wagon up onto the bridge Hannah looked between the slats of the old covered bridge; she saw that the water was quite high and swirling rather fiercely. Hannah said to Taylor, "let's give him the bath that he needs." Taylor gathered the body up in his arms and carried him to the side of the bridge. Hannah helped him lift the body over the side of the railing. They dropped Bartell's body, carpet and all, into the swirling water below. She watched as the body quickly was carried out of sight in the strong current of the water below.

Hannah turned to Taylor and said, "This is our secret. No one will ever know what happened to Bartell. He died as he lived."

Hannah got back up in the wagon beside Taylor and they headed for home. She handed him

the small gold snuffbox and suggested that he give it
to Cleo as a present.

Chapter fifty-five

Hannah went home to her farm completely at peace. She decided to burn her bloody apron in the stove. The last remnant of Bartell was gone. Besides, she had bread to bake before dinnertime. She would also be attending church tomorrow morning. She wanted to have her 'Sunday' frock pressed so that she could look her best for the pastor. When she thought about him, she got that same old warm feeling inside of her. This time, she would be able to respond differently to the pastor's attentiveness.

The following morning, when Hannah was walking out of church after the service, she leaned over to the pastor and whispered, "I've decided that I am ready to begin to live my own life again."

The pastor smiled and took her hand in his, giving it a warm handshake. "I'll be calling on you tomorrow afternoon," he said.

"That will be perfect, Ezra, shall I fix lemonade for us to share?"

THE END

Other books written by Cora A. Seaman

Keeping the Promise
(Nom de Plume)
Alyce Godbey

Emily's Quest

The Making of Mary Ann

The Roosevelt Family of Southern Illinois

A Tangled Web

Coming soon:
The Secret of the Old Stone Chapel
All About Harry

LaVergne, TN USA
15 December 2009
167059LV00004B/8/P